'How long is it ⟨since you last saw⟩ **your fiancé?'** Adam asked.

'Five days,' Petra replied.

'Five days away from the woman he loves and he just pecks her on the cheek. That strikes me as a bit odd.'

His observation made Petra defensive. 'It's not odd at all.'

'Would you like me to show you what I would have done in similar circumstances?' he asked, his voice low and husky. 'Let's pretend I'm Mark,' he said, moving a few paces away. 'I'm striding towards you. "Hello Petra, my love", is what I'd say. And then I'd do this…'

Before she could catch her breath, Adam had swept her into his arms and pulled her to him. He held her closely to his chest. Then, before she could protest, he brought his mouth down on hers…

Barbara Hart was born in Lancashire and educated at a convent in Wales. At twenty-one she moved to New York, where she worked as an advertising copywriter. After two years in the USA she returned to England, where she became a television press officer in charge of publicising a top soap opera and a leading current affairs programme. She gave up her job to write novels. She lives in Cheshire and is married to a solicitor. They have two grown-up sons.

Recent titles by the same author:

A FATHER FOR HER CHILD

ENGAGING
DR DRISCOLL

BY
BARBARA HART

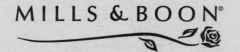
MILLS & BOON®

All the characters in this book have no existence outside the imagination of the author, and have no relation whatsoever to anyone bearing the same name or names. They are not even distantly inspired by any individual known or unknown to the author, and all the incidents are pure invention.

First published in Great Britain 2001
Harlequin Mills & Boon Limited,
Eton House, 18-24 Paradise Road, Richmond, Surrey TW9 1SR

© Barbara Hart 2001

ISBN 0 263 82700 3

Set in Times Roman 10½ on 12 pt.
03-1101-45551

Printed and bound in Spain
by Litografía Rosés, S.A., Barcelona

CHAPTER ONE

'WE HAVE a caller named John on line two. Go ahead and put your question to our medical team, John.'

The morning DJ from the local radio station flicked a switch on his control panel and a man's voice came across loud and clear. The DJ gave a thumbs-up to the two doctors sitting across the desk and mouthed the words, 'This is the last one', indicating to Petra and Adam that the radio phone-in was almost over.

'I have this problem, Doctor,' started the disembodied voice, haltingly. 'My wife's having our first baby and she wants me to be there at the birth. Now, my problem is I'm very squeamish and I'm scared that I'll make a fool of myself. You know, pass out or something.'

The DJ pointed to Petra, indicating that she should answer first.

'Hi, John, it's Dr Petra here. If your wife wants you in the delivery room with her, then I think it's a really great thing if you could put your squeamish feelings to one side and go along with her to be supportive. You can sit in at the top end, so to speak, holding her hand and helping her with the breathing and all that kind of thing. It's a most wonderful moment in both of your lives and I think you'll be sorry if you miss it.'

Adam leaned forwards towards his microphone.

'I couldn't agree less,' he said, much to Petra's

surprise. Up to now they had maintained pretty much a consistency of approach, each backing up the other in the medical advice and opinions they'd been handing out over the air for the past half-hour.

She flicked an irritated glance at Adam—why was it that there always seemed to be a degree of arrogance with good-looking men?

'If your natural instincts tell you not to be present at the birth, John, then you go along with that,' Adam continued. 'It's no use forcing yourself to do something that you feel is not for you.'

The man at the other end of the phone breathed an audible sigh of relief.

'You don't think I'm a wimp?' he asked. 'I mean, all my friends who've had children seem to have been at the birth. I was beginning to feel there was something the matter with me for not wanting to be there.'

'Be reassured, John,' said Adam, 'there's nothing wrong with you. You're probably just more honest than most of your friends. I read a survey that was carried out some years ago, asking men if they were glad that they'd been present during the birth of their children. When their partners were present they all said they were delighted they'd been there. But when the interviewer saw the fathers later by themselves, a large number admitted that although it was a remarkable and moving experience, it was one they would rather have missed.'

'Oh, really?' said John with great interest.

Petra listened with mounting exasperation—surely he could have toned down his remarks slightly? She bit her lip as he continued smoothly.

'These particular men, the ones who wished they'd

not been there, all said they were filled with admiration for the way in which their wives had coped with the delivery. But it was an image that they found hard to forget when the delivery was over and the woman was back in the marital bed. For these men, watching their babies born had a bad effect on their future sexual relationship.'

'That sounds very dubious to me!' interrupted Petra, furious that Adam had undermined her advice to John. 'Are you sure you're not making that up?'

Adam turned to face her, holding his headphones steady with one hand, pointing an angry finger at her with the other.

'I *never* make things up! I can give you chapter and verse on this particular research if you doubt my word!' He virtually spat the words out.

'We've only a little time left, doctors,' said the DJ, undecided whether it was a good thing or a bad thing that his medical team seemed to be coming to blows on air. 'So, to sum it up, John, one doctor says yes and one says no. Let us know whose advice you decided to take! And that's all from *Medical Phone-In* for today. Keep sending in your medical questions and we'll be back with Dr Adam and Dr Petra the same time next week. And now over to the newsroom for the hourly bulletin.'

When the transmission light went out in the studio, Adam and Petra each removed their headphones and pointedly ignored each other.

'I'm not sure if I wish to take part in next week's programme,' Adam said to the DJ, 'if my medical colleague is going to shout me down on air.'

'I did not shout you down!' said Petra indignantly. 'I only said what I believed.'

He turned on her angrily. 'You actually said, on air, that I was a liar. That I was lying about statistics!'

'I never said that!' Petra retorted, then, blushing, she recalled that she had almost said that—albeit in different words.

'Can you two, please, carry on your argument outside the studio?' said the DJ, concerned that by the time the news bulletin was over these two highly charged members of the medical profession would still be verbally slugging it out in his studio.

They took the hint and left the studio through the heavy, soundproofed door and carried on their animated conversation as they walked along the corridor towards the reception area.

'OK, OK,' said Petra with slight remorse. 'Maybe, in the heat of the moment, I jokingly said you might have made up that research.'

'That was a joke? You call that a joke?' Adam strode ahead of her, making her almost run to keep up with him.

'Sort of.'

'Funny sense of humour you've got, casting doubt on a colleague's honesty.'

I've got to put an end to this silliness, thought Petra as she grabbed Adam's arm, forcing him to slow down.

'Look, I've said I'm sorry. It won't happen again. What else do you want, blood?'

She looked into the brown eyes and the handsome, square-jawed face of the man she had met for the first time that morning. Dr Adam Driscoll had stepped in at short notice when the producer had decided that it would make a better programme if there were two doctors to answer the phone-in medical problems rather than just one. Dr Petra Phillips had handled the slot on her own since its inception four months ago. The producer had told her it would be a good idea—it would take some of the pressure off her and would add an extra viewpoint. She'd agreed.

It had all worked out fine during the first programme with both of them until the new doctor had jumped in and contradicted her advice to that last caller.

'Respect from a medical colleague,' he replied calmly. 'That's what I want.'

'OK,' she said, smiling her most winning smile. 'You got it!'

The way she said it, impishly with a toss of her short blonde bob, burst his bubble of seriousness and made him laugh out loud.

'That's better,' she said, squeezing his arm. On impulse she reached up and planted a kiss on his cheek. When he reacted with slight surprise at her over-friendly gesture, she just laughed.

'Just following my natural instincts,' she said. 'That's the advice you gave our last caller, wasn't it? I suppose you do follow your own advice?'

His face had begun to soften, his dark, brooding air lightening a little. Petra thought he was devastatingly attractive and found herself blushing once again under his scrutiny.

'Yes, I do,' he replied. 'I'm just a little surprised at you, that's all.'

'Girls have natural instincts, too, you know! Not just big, hunky chaps like you!' She was glad the heavy atmosphere between them had lifted. She realised, with a shock, that she was now shamelessly flirting with him—quite unsuitable behaviour for a respected general practitioner from a large inner city medical practice!

'Oh, I know girls have natural instincts. Lots of them,' he added smoothly. 'I'm just surprised at yours, that's all.'

He reached out, taking her left hand in his. A thrilling tingle run up Petra's arm and into the centre of her being as he touched her for the first time.

Then she felt him caress her third finger and the solitaire diamond ring.

'I presume this means you're engaged to be married?' he asked.

'Oh,' said Petra, startled, pulling her hand away from his.

'Men notice things like that,' he said. 'When you see a great-looking woman, it's the second thing you think of—has she got a ring on her finger?'

'The second thing you think of?' repeated Petra innocently. 'What's the first?' As she blurted out the words she could have kicked herself. How naïve could you get?

'I don't answer those kind of questions on the grounds I might incriminate myself.' Adam laughed.

Petra was now feeling rather flustered. 'Yes, well anyway, will we see you here next week for the phone-in?'

'You bet.' This time he kissed her on the cheek.

A warm, sensual glow descended on her as she watched him walk away, his body long and rangy and surprisingly graceful for one so tall. She touched her cheek where she could still feel the imprint of his lips, rough and yet at the same time soft…the kind of lips she would very much like to feel on hers.

She dropped her hand to her side. Whatever was she thinking of? Why on earth was she lusting after this man, wanting him to kiss her…and kissing him first, no less! She was engaged to Mark, for heaven's sake!

What a strange woman you are, Petra Phillips, she said to herself as she took the lift to the basement car park and drove to the medical centre for her first surgery of the day.

'Here comes the radio star,' jested Robin, one of her partners in the group practice, as they met in the car park of the medical centre.

The older man had said it every time he'd seen her in recent weeks and it was beginning to grate. She sometimes wondered if it annoyed him that it had been her name, not his, that had been put forward when their senior partner had been asked by the local radio station to suggest someone suitable for the radio show.

'I was listening on my way in,' he remarked. 'That new chap gave you a bit of a drubbing, didn't he?'

Petra blushed at the memory.

'It was probably my own fault,' she said lightly. 'I shouldn't have cast doubt on his advice…even though I did think he was wrong!'

'You young doctors, you're so impetuous,' said Robin with a smirk. 'You can still learn a thing or two from oldies like me!'

So that was it! Dr Robin Cutler was having a dig at her because she was at least twenty years younger than he was. The male menopause, she decided…and, instead of rising to his bait, she smiled demurely at him as they walked into the medical centre together.

'Morning, Dr Cutler and Dr Phillips,' said the receptionist as they entered. 'Dr Michaels has called a practice meeting at lunchtime today in his office. Can you both attend? Coffee and sandwiches will be provided.'

'How can I resist? Our senior partner's wish is my command,' said Robin to the receptionist.

'I'll be there, too,' confirmed Petra.

'Probably some more bad news about funding,' Robin muttered under his breath to Petra as they went in the direction of their consulting rooms, loud enough for her to hear but not so loud as to be heard by the dozen or so patients waiting to be seen by Petra, Robin and the two other doctors who were holding morning surgeries.

'It could, of course, be good news,' ventured Petra, determined to start her surgery in a positive mood. 'Perhaps we'll finally be taking on another partner to replace Ginny.'

Ginny was a very popular middle-aged doctor who had taken early retirement to look after her sick husband. No one suitable had yet been found to take her place and they were having to manage with a succession of locums.

An inner city medical practice wasn't everybody's cup of tea—which probably explained why it was taking so long to find a new partner—but Petra loved it. She loved the work, which she found challenging, and she loved the people, most of whom were warm and friendly. The medical centre was in one of the more deprived areas of Milchester, a large, sprawling industrial city that had made fortunes for the cotton barons of the 1800s but which was now struggling to provide jobs for all its citizens in the post-industrial age.

Petra had done her training at the city's renowned medical school and after qualifying had decided to stay on and work in the area for a few years. Her fiancé, Mark, on the other hand, hankered after the bright lights of London. He spent several days a week working at his firm's London office.

After they were married they were planning to live in the north. 'Mainly,' Mark had decided, 'because the house prices are so much cheaper.' But Petra had a sneaking feeling that when they'd been married for a year or so, Mark would be angling to move full time to London. She didn't feel happy or comfortable with the idea, but she'd put that thought to the back of her mind. Could Mark force her to give up her job in Milchester? A job and a town she loved? Well, she'd worry about that when, or if, the time came…

Mark and Petra had grown up in the same small country village and their families had known each other for years. The village was several miles from the centre of Milchester and was often referred to in the media as part of 'the stockbroker belt'…which was appropriate really, because that's what Mark was—a stockbroker. A very ambitious one.

Mark commuted to work in Milchester from his parents' large, seventeenth-century farmhouse—expensively renovated to within an inch of its life—and he also had a flat in London. Petra, on the other hand, needed to be closer to her work in case she was needed in an emergency or when she was on call, and she lived in a small town house a few minutes' drive away from the medical centre.

They were in the throes of looking for a larger house in one of the smarter suburbs and the date of their wedding would be tied in with its purchase. Mark was determined that when they were married he would be taking his bride 'to a home he could be proud of', a home where they could have friends round for dinner parties...and where he could invite his stockbroker colleagues up from London for a weekend in the country.

He rather fancied doing that. Living in the north of England could be made to sound a positive advantage, he decided, if he was able to refer to his house as his 'place in the country'. It was something he could put up with, living in the north, at least until they had enough money to buy a London house. He talked about it often enough to Petra that she knew his 'life plan' by heart. If ever she mentioned how happy she was, living and working in Milchester, Mark would get exasperated with her and act as if she were some kind of imbecile. 'How could anyone prefer living up here to living in London!' The idea was so obvious and so laughable he didn't even voice it as a question!

At lunchtime the four doctors who had been holding morning surgeries and clinics trooped into the largest consulting room which belonged to the senior partner of the practice, Dr Don Michaels. It also doubled as a meeting room.

'Glad you could all make it,' Don Michaels said affably as his partners moved to seat themselves around the small conference table which had been laid out with soft drinks, coffee and sandwiches. Petra noticed that there was an extra place setting.

'So, what's all this about, Don?' enquired Robin,

speaking the thoughts of all of them. 'Are we getting a massive pay rise?' He gave a hollow laugh as he poured himself a coffee from the large catering flask.

'All will be revealed in a moment,' replied Dr Michaels.

'Money, money, money—is that all you think of, Robin?' joked Patrick Perrott, another of the partners, a thin, red-haired doctor with glasses. Patrick was in his late thirties and in the middle of an acrimonious divorce.

'Certainly is,' replied Robin lightly. 'With three kids to get through university and a large mortgage to pay off, I can assure you that money comes a very close second to medical vocation as far as I'm concerned.'

The other partner present at the meeting was Hannah Hughes. Her age was somewhere in the early forties, a brown-haired woman who was liked on sight by almost everybody. She, more than anyone, had helped Petra to ease herself into the practice. Always encouraging and with a sympathetic ear, Petra looked on Hannah as a true friend.

As Robin and Patrick exchanged banter about who was the most in need of an injection of extra funds— Robin, with his university fees and mortgage, or Patrick, with his 'avaricious' soon-to-be-ex wife— Hannah caught Petra's eye. The two women moved to the same side of the table and sat down next to each other.

'I thought you were good on the radio today,' Hannah said. 'I managed to catch most of the show before I had to get going with the diabetes clinic.'

'Thanks,' said Petra gratefully. Although she sounded one hundred per cent in control on the air, answering all the medical questions that were thrown at her, in reality she was far from the completely confident personality that she projected. She only needed one person to say something critical—like Robin had in the car park—and she was a bundle of insecurity.

'I'm not sure how much longer I want to keep it up,' she confided in Hannah. 'It can be quite nerve-racking.'

'I hope you weren't put off by that upstart of a man who barged into your show this week! The beast!'

Petra laughed at Hannah's comical facial expression.

'Thanks for your support! I did wonder if perhaps I'd done the show for long enough—four months now. I'm not sure how the others in the practice feel about it. Perhaps it's causing a bit of…you know, resentment?'

'You mean old Robin?' Hannah lowered her voice conspiratorially. 'Take no notice of him. He's been trying to become a media star for years! Without the slightest success. All the medical journals must be sick of sending him rejection slips, yet still he keeps bombarding them with long, boring features on a whole range of topics. And now he thinks the TV channels might be interested in him. None of them return his calls. You think he'd take the hint, wouldn't you?'

Before Petra could reply, Dr Michaels tapped his knuckles on the table and said, half-humorously, 'Let's call this meeting to order.'

The room fell respectfully silent as the four doctors looked to their senior partner, curious as to why they had been asked to this extra meeting.

'As you know,' continued Dr Michaels, 'for some months now we've been working with too few doctors.' He cleared his throat.

'In a few minutes' time I'm hoping that the situation will change for the better, because I've invited a young doctor along to join us for lunch, and he has shown great interest in working here permanently.'

A murmur of approval went round the room. They had all needed to take on an extra workload since Ginny had left as the short-term locums came and went in rapid succession.

'He's a young man who comes with glowing references and was until a short time ago working in a medical team over in Bosnia, running a health centre on the edge of a war zone.'

'He'll certainly find himself at home in inner city Milchester!' remarked Patrick cynically.

The intercom buzzed and the receptionist announced that there was someone to see Dr Michaels.

'That will be him now,' he said. 'I'll go and get him.'

Dr Michaels left the room and returned almost immediately with a brown-eyed, handsome man, his dark hair cut short but not too short, a well-cut grey suit encasing his tall, well-proportioned body.

On seeing him, Petra's jaw dropped.

'It's him!' she hissed to Hannah.

'Who?'

'That man, the new doctor…it's the man I was with on the radio show this morning!' Petra's heart seemed to miss a beat.

'You mean he's that upstart who muscled in on

your radio show?' muttered Hannah between gritted teeth.

'Yes!'

Hannah leaned close to Petra's ear. 'He's a bit of a dream, isn't he?'

Petra giggled nervously, putting her hand to her face to suppress her mounting hysteria.

At first Adam didn't seem to notice her. He was too busy concentrating on taking in the roomful of strange faces that were turned towards him.

'This is Dr Adam Driscoll,' announced Dr Michaels. 'Be nice to him, because if he likes the look of us he's quite likely to be persuaded to join the practice!'

Before Adam sat down in the place reserved at the table for him, Dr Michaels formally introduced him to everyone present. When he came to Petra, she noticed that Adam's jaw dropped in the same way as hers had done a few moments earlier.

'Well, hello again,' Adam said charmingly when he'd recovered from his momentary shock.

Dr Michaels was taken aback. 'You two know each other?'

'We met for the first time today,' he explained to Petra's curious male colleagues. 'We were on a radio phone-in together.'

'So that was you, was it?' exclaimed Robin. 'You're the one who gave our young partner here a bit of a telling-off!'

'What's all this about?' Dr Michaels was out of his depth in this particular conversation.

Petra began to prickle under her armpits as she realised, with embarrassment, that she would have to explain about publicly criticising a fellow doctor on air. A doctor they were all hoping would want to become the much sought-after partner.

What would her senior partner think about her and how she'd behaved? She could see that Robin was hugely enjoying her discomfort.

Adam shot a glance at Robin and then looked back again at Petra, taking in the situation.

'It was my fault entirely,' he said addressing his remarks to Dr Michaels. 'It was my first time on a radio show and I hadn't quite got the hang of it. If anyone needed telling off it was me…I kept jumping in at the wrong time, all that kind of thing.'

Petra breathed a sigh of relief. Robin looked disappointed, having hoped there would be a few sparks flying round to liven up the meeting.

'Diplomatic as well as dishy,' whispered Hannah to Petra. 'He'll go far.'

The group settled down for an informal lunch with their prospective new partner.

'So what's all this about Bosnia?' enquired Patrick. 'Were you in the armed forces?'

'No,' answered Adam, 'I was with a group of medical volunteers.'

'That sounds exciting,' replied Patrick, 'and also a little dangerous.'

'Very dangerous. But we were kept so busy patching up the sick and wounded that we had very little time to worry about personal danger.'

'Bet you got a buzz out of being there, in the firing line so to speak,' suggested Robin enthusiastically.

'Not really,' replied Adam. 'The adrenalin stops pumping quite so fast after the first day or so. It just becomes another job. And it's not very glamorous either. The injuries you have to deal with are often horrific…and the victims, particularly the young ones…'

His voice trailed off, as if he was unwilling to go into further detail, even among medical colleagues.

'Is that why you decided to leave Bosnia and come back home?' enquired Hannah.

'No.' Adam said to the woman seated next to Petra. 'I came home for personal reasons.'

Dr Michaels turned the conversation to the more practical aspects of the inner city practice.

'I've already outlined to you the kind of work we do—the special clinics, the profile of our patients, all that sort of thing. We discussed that at our preliminary meeting. Is there anything you would like clarified now that we're all here together?'

The meeting got properly under way and Adam was able to learn more about the workload he would be expected to take on—his prospective partners keen to make the job sound as tempting as possible. They all knew they stood to gain if he joined them. They had been looking after Ginny's patients for too long and the extra work was taking its toll of all of them.

'How do you think you'll like being back in England after working so long overseas?' ventured Petra, curious to know more about Adam and his motivation for coming home.

'I think I'll like it very much,' he said, eyeing her with a piercing scrutiny that made her want to turn away in case she started to blush. But she didn't turn away. She returned his gaze unblinkingly.

'Are you from this part of the country?' she asked, surprised at her own curiosity about him. His accent gave little away and for some reason she wanted to know as much about him as possible.

'No, I'm not from round here,' he replied. 'But I have personal reasons for choosing to live up here at the moment.'

She was dying to probe further, to ask, for instance, what exactly were these personal reasons? But she was conscious of appearing to be too nosy if she did. She didn't even like to ask him if he was married. She was relieved when Hannah asked him that question instead.

'No,' he replied, 'I'm not married.'

'Count yourself lucky,' said Robin with a heavy irony that he imagined passed for humour. 'I've three kids to put through university and a huge mortgage to pay off—that's what marriage does for you!'

'Give it a rest, Robin,' said Hannah, changing the conversation to the subject of computerised medical records.

When the lunch meeting was nearing its end, Dr Michaels stood up and said, 'It was good of you to come in and spare the time to meet everyone today, Adam. After a discussion with my partners, I'll get back to you very soon.'

'Let's decide now!' said Robin. 'If Adam waits in Reception for a moment, I'm sure we can give him an answer extremely soon!'

They all agreed and Adam stepped outside for a short time.

The feeling among the partners was unanimous. Adam Driscoll should be offered the job. He was called back in.

'You may need time to think about it,' said Dr

Michaels, 'but everyone here at Milchester Medical Centre would like you to be the new GP partner.'

'I don't need time to think about it,' said Adam, grinning from ear to ear. 'Just tell me when I can start!'

As he said the words, Petra was convinced he looked at her, just for a second, before looking at her colleagues. A warm, comforting glow spread through her. Adam Driscoll would be joining her practice! She would be working with him, seeing him on a regular basis. Now, why did that give her such a thrill? Why had that just made her day?

She walked out of the medical centre with him.

'I'm just popping along the street to the newsagent's to get an evening paper,' she said as they walked along together. 'We're house hunting, my fiancé and I. I'm hoping there might be a suitable one in this evening's paper as there's a good property section in today's issue.'

When they'd walked a short distance, a black sports car pulled up alongside them and parked on the double yellow lines. A man in a dark grey pin-striped suit jumped out and strode over to Petra.

'What a surprise!' she said. 'I wasn't expecting to see you till tomorrow!'

'Change of plan,' he said briskly. 'The estate agents have sent some very exciting details through the post and I've made a provisional viewing appointment to see one of the houses today.'

Before Petra could answer, Adam roared with laughter.

'That's the first time I've ever heard of anything that could remotely be described as exciting being pushed through a letterbox by an estate agent!' The idea continued to tickle him and his infectious laughter spread to Petra who began to giggle.

'And who, might I ask, is this?' said the man bitingly.

'Oh, Mark, this is Dr Adam Driscoll,' said Petra, controlling her giggles. 'He's our new partner at the practice. And, Adam, this is Mark, my fiancé.'

Adam held out his hand to Mark who took it formally and with slight reluctance. Petra could tell that the two men were poles apart and that Mark, who took himself very seriously, hadn't been amused by Adam's reaction to his remark about estate agents.

After a brief dismissive nod in Adam's direction, Mark proceeded to ignore him and carried on talking to Petra.

'I'm in a hurry right now,' he told her. 'I'm parked on double yellow lines and I have to get back to the office. Are you able to come and see this house tonight?'

'I finish quite late tonight,' she said. 'I could pop out and see it before evening surgery.'

'I suppose that would do,' said Mark reluctantly. 'Can't you get away earlier?'

Petra shook her head.

'I've got a window between five-thirty and six-thirty,' she said, adopting his style of office-speak.

'See you at five-thirty in that case, if that's the best you can do,' said Mark, brusquely pecking her on the cheek before striding back to his car. In seconds he had revved up and driven away.

Petra and Adam stared after him for a moment.

'So that's the man you're going to marry?'

'Yes,' replied Petra.

'Hmm,' said Adam.

'What's that supposed to mean?'

'Nothing. Just…'

'Just what?' Petra felt uncomfortable, but didn't know why. Normally when she introduced people to Mark she experienced great pride in the fact that this was the man to whom she was engaged. But standing next to Adam, seeing him looking at her in such a funny way…her personal feelings were becoming all mixed up.

'How long is it since you last saw him?' Adam asked.

'Five days,' she replied. 'Mark's been in London on business.'

'Five days away from the woman he loves and he just pecks her on the cheek? That strikes me as a bit odd.'

His observation made Petra defensive. 'It's not odd at all.'

'All I can say is, if I'd been away for five days from a woman I loved,' stated Adam, 'I'd be giving her more than just a peck on the cheek.'

'Mark's not keen on public displays of affection,' said Petra, desperately trying to find a way of defending her fiancé. Deep down she did rather wish that Mark was more openly affectionate. But that's just the way some people were, she surmised. Even when they weren't in public, Mark wasn't the most tactile of men, she had to admit. More often that not it was she who would initiate what Mark referred to as 'touchy-feely stuff'. Things would change once they were married. She was sure of that. Well, almost sure of it.

'Would you like me to show you what I would

have done in similar circumstances?' Adam asked, his voice low and husky, his eyes boring into hers.

Petra was mesmerised by him. She blinked, like a rabbit caught in the beam of a car's headlights. She nodded mutely.

'Let's pretend I'm Mark,' he said, moving a few paces away. 'I've just parked my car and here I am, striding towards you. "Hello, Petra, my love" is what I'd say. And then I'd do this…'

Before she could catch her breath, Adam had swept her into his arms and pulled her to him. She was nearly—literally—swept off her feet as his arms held her closely to his chest. Then, before she could protest, he brought his mouth down on hers. Instinctively she closed her eyes and, instead of pulling away, leaned towards him. His kiss, at first, was soft and gentle, then he deepened it, pressing his lips urgently into hers. As suddenly as he had started kissing her, he stopped, pulling away and letting her go.

'That's the kind of thing I would have done if I'd been Mark,' he said, before turning on his heel and walking briskly away without a backward glance.

CHAPTER TWO

PETRA stared after Adam for a moment, gathering her wits. One or two passers-by had smirks on their faces, but most people in the vicinity ignored her, intent on their own business, wrapped up in their own affairs.

She hurriedly walked back to the medical centre, deciding that perhaps after all she didn't need an evening paper. What she needed, more than anything, was to sit down in the privacy of her own room and calm herself down. A jolt of alarm had leapt inside her as, for the second time that day, the touch of Adam Driscoll's lips on hers had sent inappropriate thrills racing through her.

Mark picked Petra up as arranged at five-thirty and they drove out of the city in a southerly direction.

'This is going to take ages,' grumbled Mark. 'I'd forgotten about the rush-hour traffic.'

When they did get to the house it meant they only had a very short time to look round it as Petra needed to be back in Milchester for evening surgery. All this put Mark in a very bad mood.

'So, what do you think of the house?' he asked. They'd just been given a whirlwind tour of the place by the estate agent and were now standing in the garden, looking at the exterior of the house.

'It's nothing special,' remarked Petra.

Mark flung his arms down by his side in exasperation. 'You say that every time! Every house we look at!'

It was true. Petra hadn't been terribly impressed by any of the houses Mark had chosen for them to look round.

'What I mean,' explained Petra, 'is that for the money they're asking, this house is over-priced. So were all the others we've looked at. They're over-priced…and nothing special.'

'This is a very sought-after area, and if we want a house in an area like this we're going to have to pay a lot of money,' reasoned Mark. 'But, of course, nothing like the money we'd have to pay in London.'

'But we could look in another area,' suggested Petra. 'A less fashionable area… We'd be able to get something much nicer and much cheaper. Perhaps we should look somewhere like the north of Milchester.'

'We most certainly will not!' stormed Mark emphatically. 'I'm not bringing my London friends up to stay in that kind of place…overlooked by old mill chimneys and all that kind of ugliness.'

'But it can be beautiful,' enthused Petra. 'All that old industrial architecture, the old mills and factories… All those old buildings are now being renovated and put to other uses. And many of the old mill towns are set among lovely hills on the edge of the countryside.'

'We're not living there, and that's definite,' stated Mark firmly. 'What would people think of us, living among the dark, satanic mills?'

'It's not like that at all! Not any more.'

'We'd be much happier if we lived somewhere like this—much more our kind of people,' insisted Mark. 'Believe me, Petra, I know about these things.'

Petra found herself secretly suppressing a smile. How many times had she heard Mark end an argument with those words? It seemed to her that he was convinced that he knew everything about everything! She was sorely tempted to make a snappy response but instead she just checked her watch, kissed him and told him that it was time she was heading back to the medical centre.

She *did* love Mark, very much—he was so kind and generous and strong. But sometimes, just *sometimes* she wished he wasn't so fixed in his ideas of what was right for them…for her. If only he could relax a little and see things from someone else's perspective occasionally.

The evening surgery was going smoothly. The patients tended to be workers who found that the later surgery hours suited them better than earlier in the day. Most patients had appointments, with the occasional one calling in on spec, hoping to be fitted in at the end of surgery or to slip in if someone hadn't turned up.

One such patient, a Mrs Gorton, came into Petra's room almost in a state of hysteria.

Petra was taken by surprise as she had always considered Mrs Gorton to be the last person who would turn up without an appointment, looking like a madwoman. Mrs Gorton, a respected pillar of the community, was the wife of a local MP and was a city councillor of many years' standing. Yet here she was, red in the face, puffing and panting, with her eyes staring wildly round the room.

'What is the matter, Mrs Gorton?' asked Petra as

she stood up and moved round her desk towards her patient.

'I think I'm having one of those panic attacks,' she gulped.

Petra could see the woman was hyperventilating and was in obvious distress.

'When does this happen?' she asked. 'Every day?'

'No. I had one about a week ago and then I had another one today,' she said. 'I was in a department store and I came over all panicky. I just had to get out. I pushed past everyone and ran out. They probably thought I was a shoplifter!'

Petra smiled, admiring the fact that the woman could still make a joke even though she was in such a state.

'Are you having an attack now?'

Mrs Gorton nodded. 'It started again when I was sitting in the surgery, waiting to see you. I was going to rush out but the receptionist kindly brought me in straight away.'

Petra noticed the shopping bag at Mrs Gorton's feet.

'Do you have a paper bag in there?' she asked.

'I think so,' replied a confused Mrs Gorton. 'I bought some apples from a street barrow earlier on.'

Petra delved among the shopping, found the brown paper bag and emptied out its contents. She then handed the bag to Mrs Gorton.

'Breath into this,' she instructed. 'Put it over your nose and mouth and just keep breathing into it.'

The woman did as instructed and within a very short time her breathing and heart rate had returned to normal. She lifted her head slowly from the paper bag, hardly able to believe that such a simple thing could have cured her.

'How on earth did that work?' she asked, mystified.

'You'd been hyperventilating and the amount of oxygen you'd taken in was greatly increased,' explained Petra. 'This resulted in a decrease in the amount of blood carbon dioxide. We needed to bring the oxygen and carbon dioxide blood level back to normal. Breathing into the paper bag did just that.'

'Simple!' laughed a relieved Mrs Gorton.

'Often the best cures are,' said Petra. 'But we need to find out why you have these panic attacks. They can be associated with a number of things, from asthma to acute anxiety. You may never get another one, but I'll just give you a check over to see if I can find an obvious cause.'

Mrs Gorton confirmed that she didn't suffer from asthma, and Petra's examination seemed to rule out several other causes.

'That leaves us with anxiety, Mrs Gorton. Is there anything that you're feeling particularly anxious about?'

Mrs Gorton didn't answer immediately. 'Not really,' she said as she bent down and replaced the apples in the paper bag.

'I'm reluctant to prescribe anything until I have a clearer picture of what might be the underlying cause of these attacks,' said Petra. 'And, as I mentioned, you may never get another one. I see from your notes that you're on HRT. If you weren't, that's something I would suggest as sometimes the menopause and the drop in hormone levels can be the cause of some kinds of anxiety attacks. Your blood pressure is normal and your chest sounds fine. So for now I suggest you try that simple paper-bag remedy if you feel an attack coming on. But these things often go away on their own. If you're still getting them in a couple of weeks' time, make another appointment to see me and we'll do some tests and possibly try some medication.'

At the end of evening surgery Petra put on her jacket and began fishing in her handbag to find her car keys. Just as she was stifling a yawn the receptionist stuck her head round the door.

'I know you're on your way home,' she said in hushed tones, as if she didn't want her voice to carry, 'but I wonder if you'd mind seeing one more person?'

Petra let her head sink onto her chest in an exaggerated expression of fatigue. It had been a long day, starting with the early morning radio show and ending with late surgery. Her show of tiredness wasn't total put on.

'He isn't a patient,' added the receptionist. 'I'll send him away if you want me to.'

She came fully into the room and pushed the door almost shut as she explained a little more about this last-minute request.

'It's a young man, in his twenties, I'd say. Something about him made me take pity on him. He's very polite and nice-mannered.'

'What does he want?' asked Petra.

'Well, that's just it. He wasn't very specific. He just said he wanted to see you and speak privately about a certain matter. He doesn't want to register as

a patient, he says, and he's very insistent that it is
you he must speak to.'

'Does he look like a druggie?' That was always
Petra's fear—that a drug-crazed addict would force
his way into the surgery and demand drugs.

'Not at all,' replied the receptionist. 'He seems a
very pleasant, well-spoken young man.'

Petra couldn't help laughing at the pleading expression on the receptionist's face.

'He's obviously very plausible, that's for sure. He
must be a right old smoothie to charm his way past
you, Sheila!' It was common knowledge that this
particular receptionist was a hard nut to crack.

Sheila smiled. 'So you'll see the lad, will you,
Doctor?'

'All right,' agreed Petra, removing her jacket and
slinging it back on her coat peg, 'but make sure you
stay close by in case I need to press the panic button.'

Sheila went out of the room, and within seconds
a young man in jeans and a sweater walked in.

'Thank you so much for agreeing to see me,
Doctor,' he said in a cultured voice. 'My name is
David Smith and I'm a research fellow at the uni-
versity.'

'Please, sit down, Mr Smith,' said Petra in a
friendly manner. Racing through her mind were a
whole variety of reasons that would explain his request for a meeting with her. Top of the list was
venereal disease. She decided he was a young man
who'd caught a dose of something nasty and couldn't
face going to his family doctor or to the university
medical centre.

So she was very surprised when he said, 'I've not
come to see you for any personal medical reason.'

He smiled nervously. 'I'm registered with another doctor, actually.'

'So how can I help you?' Petra was a little alarmed. If he didn't have a medical problem why on earth was he sitting in a doctor's surgery?

'I've been waiting outside the medical centre for quite a while,' he said, coughing nervously. 'I believe you are Mrs Andrea Gorton's doctor. Is that correct?'

Petra stiffened. What was going on? Why was this seemingly innocent-looking young man asking questions about one of her patients? Was he an undercover policeman, perhaps?

'I need to know why you're asking that question,' she replied stonily. 'All patients' records are confidential, and that includes revealing their names.'

David Smith shifted uneasily in his chair.

'I'll tell you what this is all about, Doctor, and then you can judge whether or not to help me.'

Petra nodded.

'I was adopted as a baby,' he said. 'My adoptive parents never hid the fact that I wasn't their own child. I had a very loving upbringing, and even though I was curious about my real mother I never felt the need to try and trace her. But something has happened to me recently—I won't go into the details—that has made me want to trace her.'

'I see,' said Petra.

'I've done a lot of research,' he continued, 'and I'm pretty certain that my real mother is Mrs Andrea Gorton.'

Petra's eyebrows shot up. 'We are talking about Mrs Gorton, the MP's wife? The city councillor? That Mrs Gorton?'

David nodded in confirmation.

'I even know the hospital where I was born, and her maiden name, which is Winterbottom. Her medical record would mention if she'd had a baby twenty-nine years ago, wouldn't it?'

Without thinking, Petra confirmed that it would, adding hastily, 'But, of course, the records are confidential. There's no way that I'm even going to confirm that Mrs Gorton is or isn't a patient of mine.'

'I know she's your patient,' he said stubbornly, 'because I saw her go into your consulting room. This room. I was standing outside the medical centre and looked through the window as she was called in.'

Petra bit her lip. 'That doesn't prove anything. And, anyway, why don't you speak to her direct if you're so sure she's your mother? As she's the wife of an MP, you'd have no trouble locating her address.'

'I already did,' he replied. 'I wrote to her and she wrote back saying I must have the wrong person. She said that she has never had a child "out of wedlock", as she put it.'

Petra stood up, indicating that the discussion was at an end.

'Then I'm afraid there's nothing I can do to help you, Mr Smith.'

'I know she's my mother,' he persisted. 'I just want some confirmation that she gave birth to me. I went round to her house and confronted her. She cut me dead. And when I bumped into her today in Jones's Department Store I only had the chance to get out a few words. I tried telling that I mean her no harm, but she rushed out of the shop like a thing possessed. I was worried about her so I followed her at a discreet distance to make sure she was OK. That's when I saw her come into the medical centre.'

Petra picked up her jacket and put it on.

'I'm sorry, Mr Smith, but I can't help you any further.'

A look of disappointment crossed his pale face. He shrugged his shoulders in a gesture of acceptance.

'Well, thanks anyway for your time, Doctor.' He turned and left the room.

She started looking in her handbag for the car keys, found them and then picked up her doctor's bag. She paused for a moment before leaving the room.

Something the young man had said rang a bell. Something about confronting Mrs Gorton in Jones's. She'd made no mention of that when had Petra asked her if there had been anything that could have made her anxious enough to bring on the panic attack.

Petra put down her bags and opened one of the filing cabinets where they kept the old-style records, the original patient files that had since been transferred to computer. Pulling out Andrea Gorton's file, she flicked through it. On one of the earlier, yellowing pages she read, 'Male child born in Stoneybridge Nursing Home, to Andrea Winterbottom.' Petra could tell from the date scrawled next to the words that the birth had been over twenty-nine years ago.

Closing the file, she replaced it in the cabinet and pushed it shut.

A wave of pity came over her for an instant. Pity for the young man who so desperately wanted to trace his real mother...and pity for Andrea Gorton, upstanding pillar of the community, who desperately wanted to keep secret the fact that when she'd been an unmarried nineteen-year-old she'd given birth to a baby. A baby that she'd tried to forget about for nearly thirty years.

Well, at least Petra now knew the cause of Mrs Gorton's panic attacks.

Petra drove into her town house parking space and switched off the engine with relief.

Home at last! It had been quite a day, and she was completely whacked. What she was now looking forward to was sinking into an armchair in front of the telly with a supper tray on her knees. She hadn't decided what she would have…most likely it would be one of the many frozen meals-for-one with which she'd stocked her freezer.

As she fixed the steering wheel lock and stepped out of the car, a familiar voice greeted her.

'Well, hello again! Three times in one day. Not that I'm complaining, you understand.'

She looked up quickly and to her surprise found herself gazing into the sexy brown eyes of Adam Driscoll.

'Oh!' she exclaimed, almost dropping her keys down a nearby grid.

She found herself blushing deeply and kept her head down for a few moments, pretending to be having trouble fitting her key into the lock. Seeing him standing there brought back the not-too-distant memory of their lunchtime encounter when he'd swept her off her feet in the busy street and had kissed her ardently in front of dozens of people.

'What are you doing here?' he asked pleasantly. 'Here, let me help.'

He took the bunch of keys from her shaking hands and locked the car door for her.

'What am I doing here? I live here. What about you? What you doing here?' she asked breathlessly, trying to hide the surge of excitement that was pounding through her.

'Well, fancy that!' he replied. 'I live here, too! Just moved in as a matter of fact. I'm renting number thirty-six.'

'I'm number thirty-two,' she said, suddenly wanting to laugh out loud at how she'd bumped into him three times today—and now they were going to be neighbours! Why did the thought of living next door but one to Adam Driscoll make her feel so light-hearted, so spirited…so happy?

He carried her doctor's bag for her as they walked to her front door.

'You look worn out,' he said.

'Thanks a lot!'

'I expect you've been on the go all day, starting with the radio show.' He was standing very close to her. She began to fumble again with her keys, trying to find the one that would open her front door. She wasn't normally as ham-fisted as this. But Adam was standing close to her, so close she was breathing in his warm, male scent…so close she couldn't think of anything else except how close he was! And how sexy…

'Shall I?' He took the bunch of keys once again and, finding the correct one, opened her front door for her.

'You really are tired, aren't you?' He stroked his hand gently over the silky texture of her hair.

She stepped inside, resisting the temptation to let

him carry on stroking her hair in that most soothing fashion.

'Yes, I'm tired, but I'll be fine once I've made myself something to eat and flopped down in front of the telly like a couch potato.' She smiled at him as he stood there on her doorstep, looking so handsome.

'Tell you what,' he said. 'I've not eaten yet, so why don't I go and get us a take-away pizza? I must take care of my future medical partner, mustn't I?' He placed her doctor's bag inside the hallway and before she could reply walked briskly away, calling over his shoulder, 'Pepperoni pizza with extra pepperoni? Is that OK for you?'

'Er, yes,' she replied. 'That would be great.'

When he returned half an hour later, carrying two very large pepperoni pizzas, Petra opened the door to him and led him into the small kitchen-diner.

The pine table was set with plates, cutlery and drinking glasses. And she'd made a tossed green salad which she'd put in a wooden salad bowl in the centre of the table next to a red candle. The candle had been an afterthought and, looking at it now, she wondered if it gave out the wrong kind of message. Candlelit dinners were, after all, for lovers, not for medical partners.

Adam noticed the two table settings and asked innocently, 'Just the two of us, is it? I wondered if your fiancé was going to be here so I bought the largest-size pizzas just in case.'

His words stung her, very slightly. Somehow, the fact that he thought there might have been three of them for dinner and not just a cosy twosome made Petra feel…what? Disappointed? Guilty? She couldn't put a name to the strange emotions she was experiencing whenever she was with Adam Driscoll. What was happening to her? Ever since this morning when she'd met him for the first time her reactions had gone haywire. Perhaps it was just because she was tired. Or perhaps she was finding her new medical partner just that little bit too attractive for comfort. Whatever it was, she was going to have to watch herself.

They tucked into the pizza, which was accompanied by American lager. 'Absolutely the only thing to drink with pizza,' insisted Adam.

'So tell me, how did the house-hunting go this afternoon?' he asked, cutting himself a second slice.

'Not good,' she replied. 'I'm afraid Mark and I don't see eye to eye as far as our future home is concerned.' Then, feeling she was being disloyal to her fiancé, she added, 'But I'm sure we'll find something we can both live with eventually.'

'That doesn't sound like a very promising start to a marriage,' he said lightly. 'One person forcing their viewpoint on the other.'

'Mark wouldn't force his viewpoint on me,' she said defensively, knowing full well that was exactly what her fiancé was attempting to do. 'I've probably explained it badly.'

'Let's light the candle,' he said, noticing that she'd not done so. He wasn't to know that she'd deliberately chosen *not* to light it.

'OK.' She struck a match and lit it.

'We can manage without one of these other lights now,' said Adam, jumping up and switching off the centre light, leaving just the sidelights and the candle for illumination. The room took on a totally different ambience, becoming soft-toned and seductive and more intimate.

'Tell me more about you and Mark. When are you getting married?' he asked, biting into another large slice of pizza.

'We're not sure. It all depends on finding the right house.'

'And does he live here with you? I was wondering if he might turn up later.'

'No,' replied Petra. 'He lives several miles away and commutes each day. That is, when he's not working in London.'

'Ah, yes,' said Adam. 'He'd just come back from London when we saw him today, hadn't he, when he grabbed you in that lover's embrace outside the surgery?' He winked at her over the flickering candle flame.

'Mr Peck-on-the-Cheek,' he added provocatively.

Once again the image of Adam embracing and kissing her came back to haunt her. It may have been a bit of fun for him, but it made her feel extremely uncomfortable. She put down a half-eaten slice of pizza and pushed her plate to one side.

'I think I've had quite enough,' she said.

'Are you talking about the food?'

'Not entirely.' She paused. 'I don't like the kind of remarks you keep making about my fiancé.' She glared at him for a few moments.

'It's probably time I was on my way,' he said, taking the hint.

He swallowed the last of his beer before standing up and walking to the door.

'See you in the medical centre the day after tomorrow,' he said over his shoulder.

'Is that when you start? So soon?' Her heart beat a little faster.

'Yes. Dr Michaels was desperate for me to start as soon as possible.'

He gave her a look that sent shivers down her spine. Then, with a little wave, he walked out of the house.

CHAPTER THREE

THE next day, Mark surprised her by calling in at the surgery just before lunchtime. The receptionist waved him in to see Petra between patients.

It wasn't something he often did—the medical centre was in one of the less salubrious areas of the city—and yet he'd turned up, out of the blue, on two consecutive days.

On seeing him, Petra jumped up from behind her desk and ran to him, flinging her arms around him.

'Hey, what's all this?' he said, slightly startled by her enthusiastic greeting.

'I love you, that's what,' she said, snuggling into his arms. 'We *are* engaged, you know,' she added teasingly. 'I've a perfect right to hug and kiss you whenever I want.'

Petra couldn't explain why she needed to feel his arms around her at that precise moment, or why she wanted him to kiss her...kiss her in the way Adam Driscoll had kissed her yesterday. How could she explain to the man she was about to marry that she needed reassurance...reassurance that he loved her as much as she loved him?

Mark kissed her, and for a moment she *was* reassured. A second later he pulled away.

'I've just come to tell you that we won't be able to go and view that house tomorrow—the one we talked about. The one with the conservatory. I'm afraid I've got to go to London this evening. Sorry.'

He glanced at his watch. 'And I can't stay long now I'm just on my way to meet a client for lunch at The Lemon.' He was referring to The Lemon Tree, one of Milchester's most fashionable and expensive restaurants.

Petra wasn't as disappointed at the news of Mark's imminent return to London as she imagined she should have been. She put on a sad facial expression.

'Oh, dear,' she said. 'And you've only just come back. I've hardly seen you at all for days and days.'

'I know,' he said regretfully. 'But it's work, and I don't have much say in the matter.'

She knew that wasn't entirely true. She knew how much he'd been pushing his firm to let him spend increasing amounts of time at their head office in London. But she also appreciated that it was doing his career no end of good so how could she begrudge him the opportunity?

He waved the house details at her.

'Why don't you go along and have a preliminary look at the house and see if it suits you? Then once we've crossed that hurdle we can both go and look at it. The sooner we find a house, the sooner we can fix the wedding date.'

She detected a note of criticism in his tone. Did he see her as being the main obstacle in the way of buying a house...of getting married? She sighed.

'I'd much rather we went together,' she said, not wanting to face the prospect of viewing a house on her own. Viewing a house that she already knew from the estate agent's details she wasn't going to like. It was so similar to all the others they'd seen and rejected.

'Fine.' He kissed her again, this time on the cheek.

'I'll be back in the north by the end of the week,' he said, walking to the door. Then, as if struck by an afterthought, he added, 'Or you could come down to London for the weekend and join me there. How about that? We could even check out some house prices down there just to see if they're really as horrendous as we imagine!'

He made the last remark in a light-hearted, don't-take-me-seriously way...but alarm bells rang inside Petra's head. She'd always had an inkling that Mark would try and get her to move to London as quickly as possible after they were married. Now, it seemed, he was shifting the goalposts and attempting to get her down south the moment they'd walked up the aisle.

'I'm on call this weekend,' she said, ignoring the remark about looking for a London house.

'Ah, well,' he said genially. 'I'll love you and leave you.' He blew her a kiss as he left the room, adding, 'Speak to you soon'.

When he'd gone, Petra was glad she had four more patients to see before she took her lunch-break. It meant she could put off thinking about Mark and their future together—where they would live, but more importantly the 'physical' thing.

Was Mark really in love with her? According to Adam's criteria, he didn't seem to be. He didn't grab her in a hungry embrace whenever the opportunity arose—that was true enough. It was almost as if they'd begun to take each other for granted, as if they'd become so familiar that there was no room for romantic gestures, loving words, long sensual kisses. Perhaps they'd known each other for too long, knew each other too well? When they'd been children they'd been inseparable—he'd been the first real friend she'd ever had—and even now she still thought of him as her best friend. They did love each other, of course they did. But were they actually *in* love?

It was an uncomfortable subject and she didn't want to think about it, so she pushed it to the back of her mind as the next patient was called in. He was a scruffy young man and she could see from his notes on the computer screen that he was aged nineteen.

'Hello, Jason,' she said, smiling at the sulky youth who'd come into her room chewing gum and wearing a baseball cap back to front which he made no attempt to remove—the cap or the gum.

'You're one of Dr Perrott's patients, aren't you?' she said, glancing again at the screen.

'Yeah,' he said in a surprisingly deep voice for someone so slightly built. 'He's not in today so they sent me to you.'

'And how can I help you?' she asked with a warmth she didn't feel towards this young man. His uncouth appearance was extremely offputting, but Petra had learned over the years not to judge a book by its cover. This young man could be the salt of the earth, good to his mother, kind to animals and old people and a fine example of Milchester manhood. But somehow she thought not.

'I need a sick note,' he muttered indistinctly, avoiding her eyes.

'You've had to take time off work, is that right?' she asked, tracking down the computer screen to see what the illness might be.

'I'm unemployed,' he said. 'I get benefits...but I need a sick note. Write on it that I've got a bad back.'

'And why is that?' she asked, trying to keep the suspicion she felt out of her voice. 'If you haven't got a job why do you need a sick note?'

'I was up in court yesterday,' he said, becoming aggressive now that he realised that getting a sick note from this doctor was going to be more difficult than he'd imagined. He never had any of this bother with that Dr Perrott.

'I'm sorry,' said Petra. 'I don't follow what you're saying. I still don't see why you need a sick note.'

'Because I didn't turn up in court, that's why!' Jason's red-rimmed eyes were blazing. 'My solicitor says that there's going to be warrant out for my arrest if I don't bring a sick note to say why I wasn't there.'

Petra pushed her chair back and began to get up and walk round to where Jason was sitting.

'Oh, I see,' she said. 'In that case, I'll just examine you to confirm what I'll be writing on the sick note.'

Jason jumped up as if he'd been scalded.

'You don't need to do that! Just take my word for it. I've got these really bad stomach pains.'

'I thought you said you had a bad back?'

'Just give me the bloody sick note!' Jason lunged towards the pad on Petra's desk. He knew what a sick note looked like, and if the stupid cow wouldn't write one for him he'd write it himself!

Petra put a strong restraining hand on him.

'Stop that. Immediately.' Her voice, strict and commanding, had the desired effect. Jason slunk back, cursing under his breath but retreating and leaving empty-handed.

'Nasty piece of work,' she said to herself when he'd gone. She updated his computer record, adding a warning note. 'This patient tried to get a bogus sick note to cover a missed court appearance.'

'That should spike his guns next time he tries that trick on another unsuspecting doctor,' she said with quiet satisfaction.

Later that day, as she was walking to her house from the parking area, she bumped into Adam. She wondered whether he'd been watching out for her coming home.

'Hello, neighbour,' he said. 'Busy day at the coal-face?'

'Not as bad as yesterday.' She grinned. 'That early start for the radio show made it a very long day.'

'I'll bet,' he said engagingly, matching his stride to hers as they walked along the street where they both lived. 'I'm thinking of giving it up now that we'll both be working in the same practice. The producer might find it's becoming too cosy an arrangement to have two doctors who are partners on the show together.'

'I hadn't thought of that,' said Petra.

'And, anyway, I only agreed to take part this week because I was asked by a mutual friend of mine and the producer's. I was doing him a favour.'

'Please, don't feel you have to stop because of me,' she said. 'I'm in two minds whether to carry on doing it myself.'

'In that case, let's tell them we'll do the show between us, on alternate weeks,' suggested Adam. 'Then it's not too much for either one of us. How does that sound?'

Petra thought about it for a moment.

'It sounds like a very good compromise.'

'Great!' Adam threw her an exuberant smile. It was the kind of smile that made her spirits soar and all the day's cares and woes lift from her shoulders.

They were a few paces from her door when a middle-aged woman with a small dog walked past. Petra recognised the woman as being an actress from a soap opera which was produced in the town's TV studios. Petra presumed she owned one of the more expensive, newly built town houses a few blocks away. These tended to be occupied in the week by media types who returned to their real homes at the weekends.

The small dog made straight for Adam, barking frantically. Adam, believing this to be a friendly sign, bent down and patted the dog on the head.

'Hello, nice doggie,' he said, before pulling his hand back sharply with a yelp. 'Hey, that nice doggie just bit me! Not such a nice doggie after all.'

The small dog was still barking aggressively when the embarrassed owner rushed to it and picked it up.

'You naughty boy,' she said scoldingly. Turning to Adam, she said, 'I'm most terribly sorry. I do hope he didn't hurt you. Little Rastus gets a bit nervous with strangers.'

Adam was sucking his finger where the dog had nipped him. He removed it from his mouth and looked at it. A trickle of blood oozed out of the torn skin.

'Your little Rastus has drawn blood. Look!' He pushed his finger angrily under the woman's nose. She shrank back in horror.

'Oh, my God! You'd better go and see a doctor, hadn't you?'

'I *am* a doctor,' he said squaring up to her. 'Luck-

ily for both of us I've had my antitetanus injections.
And when I say lucky for both of us, I mean that
blasted dog, not you. What we're looking at here,
lady, is a potential case of tetanus for me...' he
waved his bloody finger in the air '...and a potential
case of capital punishment for little Rastus.' He
glared menacingly at the dog which looked at him
with equal malevolence from the safety of his
owner's arms.

'Look, I really am sorry,' said the woman. 'Little
Rastus normally lives at my house in the country,
but occasionally I have to bring him into town when
I can't get anyone to look after him down there.'

'Dogs that bite are dangerous,' emphasised Adam.
'What if I'd been a small child? He could have done
a lot more damage. Dogs are allowed one bite, so
they say. Well, I reckon that little Rastus is now on
borrowed time.'

The woman walked hurriedly away, bundling her
yelping dog inside her expensive coat.

'Here,' said Petra, indicating his injured finger, 'let
me sort that out for you.'

They went inside her house and she took him
through to the kitchen. She turned on the cold tap
and Adam thrust his finger under the gushing water.

After a minute or so the puncture wound stopped
bleeding. Petra dried it with a sterile tissue and
dabbed on a small amount of antiseptic. She then
peeled the backing from a small dressing and fixed
in on Adam's finger.

'You're sure you've had your tetanus booster?'
she asked.

'Yes, Doctor.' Adam grinned. 'You don't think I'd
risk going to a war zone without it, do you?'

'Ah, yes, Bosnia.' She paused. 'So what brought you back? You said something about personal reasons?'

'Yes, that's right.'

When he didn't expand or explain any further, Petra found herself wanting to find out more about him, but got the distinct impression that to ask any more personal questions would be unacceptable.

'By the way,' she said, deliberately changing the subject. 'Did you realise you'd been bitten by Rhoda Redfern's dog?'

'And who is Rhoda Redfern?'

'Oh, come on! She's the landlady of The Railway pub in *Jackson's Market*. It's one of the most popular soaps on telly. You must have heard of it!'

'I've heard of *Jackson's Market*,' he replied, 'but never watched it.'

'Well, that's who the dog's owner is. She's a good actress.'

'Not a good dog owner, though, is she? If she knew little Rastus had a tendency to bite then she should only take him out muzzled.' Adam waved his bandaged finger at her. 'And because Ms Redfern didn't muzzle him, I shall be starting my first day at my new practice with a finger looking like this. I don't suppose it will inspire my new patients with confidence, will it? I'll have to keep one hand under the desk!'

He was only joking, but Petra could see that he was annoyed.

As he left her house she began to wonder if he was annoyed because of the dog bite or because of her inquisitive questioning. What had he got to hide?

Why was he so evasive with her and why wouldn't he level with her about those 'personal reasons'?

And why was she so curious anyway?

'Blast the man,' she muttered as she went back to the kitchen. There was something about Adam Driscoll that had got under her skin. She was becoming obsessed with him, wanting to know every detail about him even though she'd only met him yesterday.

Perhaps the 'personal reasons' had something to do with a woman, she speculated. A girlfriend, or a former wife. He'd told them at his interview that he wasn't married...but that didn't rule out having been married in the past.

She was still thinking about him as she settled down to watch some mindless television programme. And he was still in her thoughts a few hours later as she switched off the bedside light. As her head hit the pillow she began to relive, once again, the moment when his lips had touched hers and how good it had felt, how sensual and thrilling. She tried substituting Mark's face, but it didn't work...it didn't work at all. And so, feeling guilty, she gave in to her natural instincts—a phrase which reminded her even more of Adam and their first encounter—and let her dreams take over as she drifted off to sleep.

Adam's first day at the practice started well enough. Dr Michaels had offered to ease him in gently with only a few patients and a few home visits, but Adam had insisted on hitting the ground, running, by taking on his full share of the work straight away.

Within a very short time he had charmed the receptionist and the practice nurse who were falling over themselves to help him in any way they could.

'Another coffee, Dr Driscoll, or perhaps a cup of tea?' asked Sheila for the third time that morning.

'She doesn't run around like that after me,' complained Patrick, who happened to be passing at the time.

'I was just as helpful to you when you were new here, Dr Perrott,' retorted Sheila. 'Anyway, poor Dr Driscoll has a poorly finger. Bitten by a dog, he was.'

After morning surgery Adam was about to set out on his rounds and was walking to the doctors' car park. He was glancing at a street map given to him by Sheila on which she'd marked the roads where the home-visit patients lived. He was a few metres from his car—a cobalt blue sports car, which he'd bought a few months previously and which was his pride and joy—when he heard the sound of glass being smashed.

He looked up from the map and saw a youth in a black woollen hat run from behind his car and rush past him, pushing something inside his anorak as he went. His car window on the passenger side was broken.

'I'll bet that's my new stereo!' he fumed, dropping the street map and immediately giving chase. He followed the fleeing youth out of the car park and into the street outside the medical centre.

The boy moved across the pavement with stunning speed, dodging between startled pedestrians and onlookers, with Adam in hot pursuit. He was young and agile but not half as fit as Adam who began gaining on him.

On reaching a set of traffic lights which had just

turned to red, the thief paused for a second before plunging across the road. As he got to the other side he looked round quickly and, seeing Adam close on his heels, darted off in a different direction, disappearing down a small side street. But Adam was right behind him and, flinging himself at the lad's heels, brought him down in a flying rugby tackle.

The car stereo flew out of the boy's anorak and smashed into a thousand pieces on the tarmac road.

The boy struggled and writhed with a strength that was out of all proportion to his size in an effort to escape from Adam's grasp. They were both panting from the exertion, but Adam was taller and stronger and could have held onto him for a good while longer—even if the two policemen hadn't turned up in their patrol car at that most convenient moment.

'Hey, what's all this?' one of them called out as they came running towards them. They hauled Adam off his captive and pulled them both to their feet.

The boy was still kicking and struggling, but when he caught a glimpse of the police uniforms he stopped and went limp as if he knew the game was up. But he was cannier than Adam thought. As the officer began to question them, the youth pointed to Adam accusingly.

'It was him. He started it. He was beating me up! Arrest him, not me!' he spat out venomously.

'You little liar!' responded Adam angrily. 'You've just broken into my car and nicked my new stereo!'

'I never!' he yelled back.

Adam pointed to the smashed remains of his very expensive car stereo which was now strewn all over the alleyway.

'So what do you call that?' he said accusingly. 'I

heard you break my car window and saw you running away. And you had that stereo stuffed inside your coat. I'd call that caught red-handed!'

'It's all right, sir, we know this young man. We know him very well,' intervened one of the police officers.

While Adam was fuming at the whole situation the police were handcuffing the youth to make sure he didn't slip away out of their custody.

'Just a minute, officers,' Adam said, noticing blood on the thief's hands and shards of glass glinting in the sunlight. 'I think we'd better give this fellow some medical attention. Look at his hands and wrists. There's glass all over them and he seems to have cut one of his veins.'

'That's because of your frigging car window!' snarled the boy. Then he looked down at his hands, and seeing the amount of blood that was pouring all over the handcuffs and dripping onto his jeans, began to panic. 'I'm bleeding to death! I'm frigging bleeding to death!'

'You won't bleed to death,' said Adam. 'I'm a doctor. Officer, I suggest we take him back to my surgery, which is round the corner, and I can remove the glass and stop the bleeding before you take him away to the police station.'

All four of them got into the police patrol vehicle and drove the short distance to the medical centre.

'Raise your hands,' instructed Adam.

'What's this?' jeered the youth. 'A bloody hold-up?'

'If you don't want to bleed to death before we get to the surgery, then do as I tell you. All you have to do is to raise the cut above your heart level and the

bleeding will stop,' snarled Adam. He'd had quite
enough of this wretched boy for one day. He'd dam-
aged his car and stolen his stereo, and now he was
giving him cheek!

As the handcuffed youth, police officers and Adam
traipsed into the medical centre Petra was just coming out of her room. She stopped dead in her tracks.

'Jason!' she gasped, staring at the bedraggled,
blood-splattered specimen who was being frog-
marched into the room next to hers.

'You know him?' asked a surprised Adam.

'He's one of our patients, Jason McDonagh.
What's happened?'

'I caught him breaking into my car and stealing
my stereo,' replied Adam.

'Allegedly.' Jason smirked. 'I know my rights!
You've got to prove it in court first. And I want to
see my solicitor. Ouch!'

'Sorry, Jason,' said the officer to whom he was
handcuffed, 'did I just jolt you accidentally?'

As they went into Adam's room, Petra fixed Jason
with a furious look.

'Why did you do it, Jason? Why target our car
park? You know that all the cars in it belong to doctors. We need them for emergencies…you're putting
lives at risk by going for our cars. And I'm sure you
realise that no drugs are kept in them, so why do it?
To your own doctors?'

Jason eyed her vindictively. 'I thought it might be
your car. I hoped it was, anyway.'

Petra was shocked. 'But why? What have you got
against me?'

'You wouldn't give me that sick note, would you?'

He sneered. 'I wanted to give you a bit of grief, like you gave me.'

Adam, who'd been washing his hands before pulling on a pair of latex gloves, had overheard this unpleasant exchange. He saw the distressed look on Petra's face.

'He's got glass in his wound,' he said bluntly. 'I'm going to remove it before our ex-patient gets removed to the police station.'

He kept his voice expressionless, not able to trust himself to speak normally. If that youth says one more thing, he vowed, I'll punch him in the mouth and to hell with the glass in his wound.

CHAPTER FOUR

'DON'T worry about it. I understand. See you on Friday, then.' Petra replaced the receiver. That was the fourth time in as many weeks that Mark had phoned to say he'd been unavoidably kept in London. He was now spending virtually all his time down there, only returning north for one or, at the most, two days at a time.

Petra was getting used to not having him around. Sometimes she looked at her engagement ring and wondered if it was just another piece of jewellery. It was a lovely ring, an antique-cut diamond which had belonged to Mark's grandmother. Mark hadn't actually asked Petra to marry him, not formally, that was. One day, almost a year ago, he'd shown her the ring and as she'd been admiring it he'd said 'Let's get engaged.' And that had been that.

They seemed to spend all their free time looking at properties. Every estate agent for miles around had them on their mailing lists, and Petra now felt that she'd got to the stage that if she saw another brochure or set of house details she'd puke. Fortunately, for the past month Mark had been so busy with his work in London that he hadn't seemed to have had the time or the inclination to go house-hunting either.

Petra had also been very busy in the past few weeks. A minor flu epidemic had kept the surgery full, and she'd decided to slap a coat of paint on the spare bedroom which was at the front of the building overlooking the street.

One Sunday afternoon she was concentrating on painting the window-frame, trying not to get too much paint on the glass, when she saw a car pull up outside Adam's house. A woman got out and the first thing Petra noticed were her long, shapely legs which were very much on show as she leaned into the back of her car.

With one eye on her paint brush and the other on the woman, Petra watched as she pulled her seat forward to let out a small child from the back seat. It was a little boy who looked four or five years old.

At that moment Adam joined them on the pavement and Petra nearly dropped a large blob of gloss paint on the carpet as her curiosity began to get the better of her. In the month that Adam had been working at the practice he had let out very few details of his private life. Petra even began to wonder if he knew anybody at all in Milchester, apart from the friend who'd fixed him up with the radio show. So who was this very glamorous woman Adam was now greeting?

Petra noted that he only touched her lightly as he gave her a kiss on the cheek. Obviously not a girl-friend or lover! she thought to herself. Then Adam turned his attention to the little boy. He picked him up lovingly, hugging the child to him.

Petra eased the window open a little more, ostensibly to paint around the casement. Sounds drifted up from the street below—squeals and laughter from the child and occasional words from Adam and the woman. She distinctly heard Adam say, 'How's my best little boy? We're going to have such fun today!'

Then he said to the woman, 'Pick him up when it suits you.'

'Six o'clock all right?' said the woman. Then she said something to Adam that Petra didn't quite catch, before saying, 'Be good for Dadda, won't you?'

'He's always good for me,' said Adam, holding the child confidently in his arms as they both waved goodbye to the woman.

Petra put her paint brush down. Her hands were shaking and she knew it would be useless trying to paint a straight line at the moment. What had she heard? 'Be good for Dadda'? So! Adam had been married, or at least had been in some kind of relationship which had produced a child. Petra's mind was racing. 'Personal reasons.' That's why he'd returned from Bosnia, that's why he was now living in Milchester. Obviously the personal reasons had something to do with his former wife and their child. But why on earth couldn't he have said so? Why did he have to be so secretive when everyone else in the practice was quite open about their family relationships? It really annoyed her...

She studied herself in the full length mirror on the bedroom wall.

'No,' she said to her reflection. 'You're not just annoyed, are you? What you are, Petra Phillips, is jealous!'

Observing Adam with that beautiful woman, seeing him hold her child so lovingly, had brought out powerful emotions in her.

'Pull yourself together,' she ordered. 'You're engaged to someone else. You shouldn't be having these kinds of feelings about another man.'

* * *

All day she couldn't get the image out of her mind. The image of Adam and his child. She day-dreamed as she was doing the painting, pretending that the little boy was hers and that Adam was the father…and that the three of them lived together…

'I wish Mark were here,' she said out loud as she cleaned the paintbrushes in the kitchen sink. At least if he were here and they were busy viewing houses she'd have no time to be having these treacherous thoughts about another man!

As the hands of the kitchen clock moved towards six, curiosity had taken hold of her again and she made her way upstairs in order to peer down into the street to see if the mystery woman would come to pick up her child.

She arrived a couple of minutes later. Adam and the little boy came out to meet her, the child clutching a bag full of goodies which he proceeded to show to his mother.

'Dadda spoils you, doesn't he?' Petra heard her say.

Then, as the child got into the back of the car, Petra heard Adam say to the woman, 'I couldn't bear losing him.'

The woman muttered something into her hand, almost as if she was crying. Adam put a comforting hand on her shoulder.

'Well, I'm back now,' he said. 'And I'll always be here…for both of you.'

Petra jerked back from her vantage point at the window, concerned that Adam might look up and see her spying on him.

What did all that mean? Was Adam planning on getting back together with his wife?

She was still brooding about Adam and his secret family when there was a knock on the door. She opened it to reveal the smartly dressed figure of her actress neighbour, Rhoda Redfern, clutching a handkerchief to her cheek.

'I'm sorry to bother you,' she said, 'but I was looking for that doctor…the one who was nipped by little Rastus.'

'Dr Driscoll, you mean?'

'I don't recall hearing his name, but I remember that you took him into your house to deal with his cut.'

'That's right,' confirmed Petra, wondering what all this was leading to. 'He's fine now, if that's what you're concerned about.'

As she was speaking, she saw Adam coming out of his house dressed in tracksuit pants and sweatshirt. She waved to him and called him over. 'Here he is now to prove it to you himself!'

Rhoda Redfern seemed relieved to see him walking towards them.

'I'm so glad your finger's better,' she said.

'Right as rain.' He held up the now healed digit.

Petra, glancing again at Rhoda, noticed that there was blood seeping through the whiteness of the handkerchief the actress was pressing to her cheek.

'Do you know you're bleeding?' she said with concern.

'Yes. That's why I came round to try and find a doctor.' Rhoda was beginning to shake a little. 'You see, I've just been bitten by little Rastus on my face! Not badly, I don't think, but I'm due to do some filming tomorrow…and…'

'Come inside,' said Petra, putting a gentle hand on the woman. 'I'm also a doctor.'

They sat Rhoda down and, after washing their hands, took a good look at her cheek.

'That's quite a nasty bite,' said Adam. 'Another inch further up and it would have been your eye.'

'But it was only a little nip!' protested Rhoda.

'How did it happen?' Petra asked her.

'It was all my fault,' said Rhoda, her whole demeanour now totally lacking the veneer of confidence she'd previously shown. 'After little Rastus nipped you, Dr Driscoll, I decided he was far too nervy, living in town. So I gave him one of my tranquillisers crushed up in his dinner. They're not really tranquillisers, more a sort of pep pills—they keep me going when I've a long day's work ahead.'

'You gave your dog some of your own prescribed medicine?' Adam was astounded. 'You could have killed him, you know. Human medicines can be highly poisonous to animals—ask any vet.'

'Well, they didn't kill him,' she said guiltily. 'And they worked fine for a week or so. Then today he went berserk, rushing round the place, yapping and snapping at ordinary, everyday objects in the house.'

'He was probably hallucinating,' said Adam, appalled at the woman's recklessness.

'I picked him up a few minutes ago to try and calm him down and he went for my face.'

'Have you had an antitetanus injection in the last ten years?' asked Petra.

'I can't remember,' replied Rhoda. 'I had one years ago, but—'

'When we've dealt with the bite we'll give you a booster injection just to make sure. And there could be a possible problem with bacterial infection—an animal's mouth is heavily populated with bacteria that thrive on food residue.' Petra didn't want to frighten the woman, but on the other hand she needed to make her aware of the potentially serious nature of any wound made by an animal.

'The tissue damage isn't as bad as it could have been,' Adam said to Petra as the two doctors cleansed the wound, which had now stopped bleeding, and examined it.

'Will I have a scar?' asked Rhoda nervously.

'Perhaps a small one,' said Petra as she applied antiseptic. 'Fortunately you won't need stitches. In any event, with a dog bite, we much prefer to leave the wound open if at all possible. Closing it tends to encourage any bacteria that might have been transmitted by the bite to multiply. So, as well as giving you an antitetanus jab, we'll give you a prescription for some antibiotics as a preventative measure. Are you allergic to any antibiotics?'

'Not that I'm aware of,' answered Rhoda, who was looking at her reflection in a small handbag mirror. She recoiled in horror.

'I look terrible!' she cried. 'What on earth will the producer say tomorrow when I turn up looking like this?'

'Perhaps they could write it into one of the episodes of *Jackson's Market*?' suggested Adam, very much tongue-in-cheek. But the idea struck Rhoda as brilliant.

'Hey, Doc, that's not half bad! I'll phone the producer today and warn him that we'll need an extra scene—one where I get my face beaten up in a dramatic pub brawl, or...' she was really warming to the idea and now saw her injury as a creative opportunity '...one of my customers at The Railway sticks a glass in my face! The make-up department will have a field day!'

'What's going to happen to little Rastus?' asked Adam, concerned that the dog was still around to bite others. 'We might have to report this to the police.'

'Oh, please, don't, please, don't,' begged Rhoda, tears filling her eyes. 'I know you said when he nipped you that Rastus was on borrowed time, but...can't you see? It has been all my fault! If I hadn't brought him to live in Milchester he wouldn't have become nervy...and if I hadn't given him my pills... If you report him to the police they'll take him away and put him down! Little Rastus! He's my life!' She dabbed at her eyes. 'It's not as if he's bitten a stranger this time. It was only me, his owner. So it doesn't count, does it?'

Adam was aware that Rhoda was using all her acting skills in an effort to persuade him not to get her dog taken away. She was a good actress, he had to hand it to her! He could feel his resolve weakening.

'If I don't tell the police, how can we be sure he won't bite again? It could be a child or a baby next time.'

'I promise I'm on my way to buy a muzzle right now! Then I shall take him straight to the vet's to have him checked over.' Her eyes never left Adam's face. 'And the vet can keep him for a day or so until the pills have worked their way through his system. Then I'll do what I should have done in the first place, which is to get some canine medicine for him. And then—this I promise you, Dr Driscoll—I'll take him back to the country and arrange for him to be looked after in my own home when I'm not there. Now,' she said, beaming confidently at Adam, 'how does that sound?'

Before he could answer, Rhoda turned her best smile on Petra and asked her, much to her surprise, 'Do you like the theatre?'

'Er, yes,' she replied, slightly taken aback by this change of subject.

Rhoda dived into her handbag and produced two tickets.

'Would you like these?' She thrust them at her. 'They're for the latest production at the Coppock— unfortunately I'm not able to go. They're the best seats in the house. Would you and Dr Driscoll like to use them…be my guest?'

Milchester's Coppock Theatre was internationally renowned for its award-winning productions, and seats were hard to come by—and very expensive. Petra looked at Adam for guidance before accepting the tickets. Would he see it as a bribe? To her relief he was smiling and obviously prepared to drop his threat to shop little Rastus to the cops.

'That's very kind of you, Rhoda,' she said. Looking at the date on the tickets, she said to Adam, 'They're for tomorrow night. Can you make it?'

'I can, if you can,' Adam replied.

'Yes, I'm free tomorrow night,' said Petra. 'I'm not on call or anything.'

She thanked Rhoda for the tickets. All the way to the door the actress kept repeating her promise to get Rastus a muzzle and to take him straight to the vet.

As she walked away, Adam said, almost to himself, 'I just hope we've done the right thing in not reporting the dog.'

'I'm sure we have,' said Petra. 'That woman isn't going to risk any more trouble with little Rastus or she'll know it will be all over the front pages of the tabloids.'

Feeling almost elated, she waved the tickets with false jollity at Adam. 'Freebies for the theatre! Don't often get something like that given to us, do we?'

'You mean we don't often get bribed quite so blatantly?' He laughed, taking them from her. 'Let's have a look what they're for.'

'You don't really see it as a bribe, do you?' she asked anxiously.

'Relax,' said Adam. 'I was only joking. I don't feel under any obligation to the lady and if I see little Rastus round here again, unmuzzled, I'll have no hesitation in reporting the incident to the police.'

'Oh, right,' said Petra with relief. 'Me, too!'

'This should be good,' said Adam, scrutinising the tickets. 'They're for the latest David Hare play. It's had terrific reviews. It starts at 7.30. Shall we eat before or after the show?'

Suddenly Petra realised what she'd got herself into. She had, in effect, agreed to go out on a date with Adam when she was engaged to Mark. She decided she'd better backpedal a little.

'Oh, I think we'll just go to the play, shall we?' She tried to make her voice sound casual. 'No point in spending money on an expensive meal, is there?'

'Nonsense,' replied Adam, putting the tickets down on the hall table. 'These haven't cost us anything, after all. It will be my pleasure and privilege to treat my new partner to a meal out. I'll book a table at The Lemon Tree for an after-theatre supper.'

And before she could say anything he'd gone out through the front door and was continuing his jog along the pavement.

Petra knew she should have mentioned it to Mark when they spoke on the phone later that evening. But she didn't. She'd been rehearsing what she'd tell him. 'I'm going to a play with a colleague from work—and then we're having a meal.' No, that didn't sound right. 'I've been given some free theatre tickets and this chap from the practice, you've met him actually...' No, that didn't sound any better.

The problem was, although she was telling herself that the date with Adam was nothing of any importance, deep inside she felt differently about it. From the moment it had been suggested she'd begun to feel disturbingly excited at the idea of going out with him. Every time she thought about it her heart gave a little flutter and she had to make a conscious effort to stop herself from starting little fantasies about him.

She knew she was betraying Mark in her mind, if not in her body. But she said nothing, not even when Mark asked if she was planning to do 'anything interesting' while he was away in London. By that he usually meant was she going home to see her parents? The last thing he would have expected her to reply was, Yes, as a matter of fact, I'm going to the theatre tomorrow with an incredibly sexy man and afterwards he's taking me for an intimate supper at The Lemon Tree.

Of course she didn't say anything of the kind. She just replied, 'No, nothing interesting...'

*   *   *

The Coppock Theatre was an exceptional structure, a modern theatre-in-the-round designed within the beautifully restored interior of a former Victorian cotton mill. The tiered rows of comfortable seats gave the audience an impressive view of the stage, and the clever lighting and overhead gantries made for apparently effortless scene changes. Actors and audiences alike were strong in their praise of the theatre and productions were nearly always sell-outs.

'We're very lucky to have been given the tickets, aren't we?' said Petra, surveying the full house as she snuggled down into her seat with excited anticipation.

Adam squeezed her arm as the lights were dimming. 'Yes, we're very lucky.'

It was the only time he touched her during the performance, but sitting so close to him, breathing in his warm, male scent, it made Petra constantly aware of his vibrant presence.

Afterwards they walked to the restaurant which was near the theatre. Petra had only been to The Lemon Tree once before. Mark had taken her there on her birthday last year, and she had a sneaking feeling that he'd put it on expenses…it had been the way he'd deliberately picked up the restaurant receipt and stuck it in his wallet.

'Good job we booked,' said Adam as the waiter led them through the crowded restaurant to their table.

Over a plateful of succulent smoked salmon Adam repeated what he'd said at the theatre.

'I feel very lucky,' he said, his eyes fixed on her through the soft candlelight. 'Lucky that I got bitten by little Rastus!'

'That's a strange thing to say,' replied Petra. 'I wouldn't call that particularly lucky!'

Adam reached out and momentarily touched her hand. 'We wouldn't have been given the theatre tickets if his owner hadn't felt so guilty about it. And I wouldn't be sitting here with you…'

He was definitely flirting.

Petra took a long, deliberate sip of her wine, uncertain how she should respond. All kinds of feelings were mixed up inside her. As she put down her goblet, the light from the candle shone on the diamond on her engagement ring, making it glint and sparkle like a brilliant star. Adam noticed her staring at it.

'What are you thinking about?' he asked gently, his eyes fixed on her. 'Do you wish you were here with Mark instead of me?'

His words brought her down to earth.

'What kind of question is that?'

'I just wondered if you wish it was Mark sitting opposite you now instead of me. It's a perfectly normal question.'

'I'm engaged to him,' she replied, 'whereas you are I are just…partners. Nothing else.'

'That's right,' he said, reaching for her hand once again. 'We're "just partners". So why do you tremble whenever I touch you?'

She pulled her hand away, almost knocking over her wineglass.

'I don't!' she protested, going pink.

'I'm not complaining,' said Adam with a playful smile. 'It's just something I've noticed, that's all.'

'You're imagining it,' she retorted. 'Anyway, what are you trying to suggest? That I fancy you or something? Just remember, Adam Driscoll, I'm engaged to marry Mark!'

'How can I forget?' he replied. 'It's something that's constantly on my mind!'

The jokey way he said it made it difficult for Petra to decide whether or not he was being serious. Was Adam really bothered that she was engaged to another man, that she was out of bounds, so to speak? Or was he more concerned with renewing his relationship with the glamorous woman who was the mother of his child?

In any event, there was little point in pursuing the matter, Petra decided. She was going to marry Mark and therefore the details of Adam's private life didn't matter one way or the other. She changed the subject.

It was a warm evening so instead of getting a taxi home from the restaurant they decided to walk.

Petra was relieved that Adam seemed to be deliberately leaving a gap between them as they strolled homewards through the city streets. Ever since she'd agreed to go out with him she'd been worrying about how she would react if, at some time during the evening, he put an arm around her.

But here they were, almost home, and Adam hadn't attempted to lay a finger on her, let alone a whole arm. In fact, the only times he had made physical contact with her had been when he'd squeezed her arm as the theatre lights had dimmed and a couple of light touches during the meal.

'We should do this more often,' he said as they neared the top end of their road. 'Seeing as we're neighbours. It would be a sociable thing to do, don't you think?'

'Why not?' she answered lightly. 'We could arrange a meal out with the other partners from the practice if you like.'

'That wasn't what I had in mind,' he responded, touching her arm and sending an electric charge through her body. 'I meant just the two of us, like tonight.' His dark eyes softly caressed her face.

'But there's Mark,' she said. 'What would he say, I wonder?'

'What did he say this time?' asked Adam.

She looked away and pretended she hadn't heard the question.

'You didn't tell him, did you, Petra?'

'No.'

He turned her face to his. 'Why didn't you tell him?' he asked huskily. 'What did you have to hide?'

'Nothing,' she said, almost in a whisper.

'What did you think might happen?' he asked meltingly.

'Nothing,' she repeated.

Slowly, he put his arm around her and pulled her to him, one hand stroking her silky hair. She didn't resist. Instead, she leaned into him and her heart quickened. She was deeply conscious of his body and the way she could feel him stirring with arousal. She knew she could be getting herself into deep water but she was powerless to do anything except stay in the enclosure of his arms.

'Did you think this might happen?' he asked softly in her ear.

It was as if she were mesmerised, rooted to the spot. Heat burned under her skin as she heard his breathing quicken. The powerful emotion that surged through her body was extremely disturbing and, at the same time, deeply thrilling.

She didn't answer him because she didn't know what to say. She didn't want to admit that, yes, she had thought this might happen. She had wondered, or possibly even hoped, that she would end up in his arms. And how could she justify those kind of treacherous thoughts?

'Is this why you didn't tell your fiancé you were going out tonight with another man?'

At the mention of the word 'fiancé', Petra felt as though a bucket of cold water had been thrown over her. Almost with relief she found the strength of mind to disentangle herself from Adam's embrace.

'I didn't tell him because I didn't think it was important,' she replied, striding out ahead of him. She stopped walking only when she reached her front door.

'I won't ask you in for a coffee, if you don't mind,' she said, trying to sound casual even though she was shaking inside. 'Busy day tomorrow.' Giving him a quick wave, she quickly opened her front door and stepped inside without a backward glance.

Leaning against the closed door, she could feel her heart pounding.

'Phew, that was a near thing,' she muttered to herself, aghast at how close she'd come to flinging caution to the wind and giving in to her basic instincts. She ran her thumb over her engagement ring, adding, 'Sorry Mark.'

CHAPTER FIVE

'OUR practice meetings are much better these days, have you noticed?' Hannah said to Petra as they were waiting to be joined in the meeting room by the other partners. 'Certainly more interesting.'

'I suppose they are,' agreed Petra, who'd also noticed the way the regular weekly sessions had recently become less rambling and more focused. Previously the partners' meetings had tended to degenerate into opportunities for Robin and Patrick to air their own personal financial and marital problems.

'Our new Dr Driscoll can be thanked for that, I'm sure,' said Hannah, who made no secret of her admiration for Adam. 'He can cut through the waffle and get straight to the point. It was a great idea of his to include case conferences, don't you think?'

'I agree,' replied Petra. 'It helps enormously to have other partners' views on how to manage a particular case...'

Just at that moment all the other doctors arrived and seated themselves around the small conference table. Don Michaels chaired the meeting as usual.

When he'd gone through the agenda in front of him and had made one or two announcements, he asked if anyone had any patient problems they would like to discuss.

Adam spoke first.

'I've got a new patient. I mean, he's new to the

practice as well as being new to me. He was with another practice on the other side of the city but this one was more convenient. Anyway, he's suffering from acute myeloid leukaemia. He was first diagnosed two years ago and was initially treated with chemotherapy which got him into remission. Sadly for the young man, he's now relapsed and there's a problem with the next stage of his treatment.'

'How old is he?' enquired Hannah.

Adam checked his notepad. 'Twenty-nine.'

'Then he's obviously an ideal candidate for a bone marrow transplant, if a good match can be found,' said Hannah.

'Surely that will have been gone into with his specialist haematologist?' ventured Don. 'It's not for us as general practitioners to be advising the best course of treatment for him.'

'That's right,' said Adam. 'His specialist has advised exactly that course of action—that my patient should have a bone marrow transplant as soon as possible. He's still in reasonable health and the outlook for him is very good. That is, if he can get a good tissue match.'

'Obviously a close relative would be best,' stated Hannah.

'Let's hope he's in luck,' added Patrick. 'No doubt his parents and any siblings will have been tested to see if their tissue types match.'

Adam shook his head.

'Why ever not?' demanded Robin. 'The specialist wants to get his act together and get a move on. The longer the patients has to wait, the more chance of his condition worsening and the less chance he has of the transplant being a success!'

'That's the problem I was telling you about,' said Adam. 'He's adopted. There's no one that he knows who's genetically related to him. Except—'

'Oh, the poor young man,' said Hannah. 'Is he on a register for a matching bone marrow donor?'

Adam nodded. 'The specialist arranged that straight away. But he's been waiting for several months without finding one. And as we know, a match may not be found until it's too late.'

A strange feeling of recognition came over Petra as they were discussing the case of the young man with AML. 'You said he has no one genetically related to him except…except who?'

'I was going to say except his mother,' Adam replied. 'At least, there's someone whom he believes is his real mother. He desperately keen to get in touch with her, as you can imagine.'

'And who does he think is his real mother?' asked Petra tentatively, believing she already knew the answer.

Adam checked his notepad again. 'One of our patients, a Mrs Andrea Gorton.'

The other partners, apart from Petra, stared at Adam in open-mouthed amazement.

'You mean Councillor Mrs Gorton?' asked Robin. 'The scourge of unmarried mothers who try and get council flats? That Mrs Gorton?'

'The MP's wife?' chorused Patrick and Hannah.

'That's astonishing!' said Don.

'It's true,' said Petra quietly. 'I had the young man in my surgery a few weeks ago, although he didn't tell me he'd got leukaemia. He asked me to look in

Mrs Gorton's medical records and confirm that she was his mother. I told him I couldn't do that.'

'I know,' said Adam. 'That's why he asked to be registered with me as he knew there would be a conflict of interest if he became one of your patients.'

'Why would there be a conflict of interest?' asked Don. 'We often treat members of the same family without any problems arising.'

'But my patient, Mrs Gorton, refuses to accept that Adam's patient is her son,' explained Petra. 'He's already contacted her and she denied being his mother.'

'And *is* she his mother?' asked Adam. 'That's the main reason I brought up the case at this meeting.'

'She could well be,' replied Petra. 'I checked it on her medical records. Andrea Gorton gave birth to a baby boy when she was nineteen and unmarried.'

There was a loud intake of breath. 'Not such a paragon of virtue after all,' said Robin. 'I suppose she now wants to forget all about her little fall from grace.'

'She's wanted to forget all about it for twenty-nine years,' said Petra, not unkindly. 'Having given up her baby for adoption, she probably thought she'd hear no more about it. She certainly didn't expect him to come searching for her now that she's a respected leader of the community, married to a high-profile Member of Parliament.'

'We're in a bit of a pickle here, aren't we?' said Hannah. 'I can sympathise with the poor woman who finds that her past has come back to haunt her. I also feel desperately sorry for the young man whose life now hangs in the balance.'

Adam fixed Petra with a penetrating look. 'Will

you speak to Mrs Gorton about this or would you like me to do it?'

'You mean, tell her that we know she has an illegitimate son or tell her that he needs a bone-marrow transplant?'

'Both.'

Petra started to make a few notes on the pad in front of her. 'I'll talk to her today if I can contact her.'

'Excellent,' said Adam. 'There really is no time to lose.'

'It's not going to be easy,' she replied swiftly. 'I've got to drop two bombshells on her at the same time.' She tapped her pencil on the pad as she worked out her plan of action. 'Before I phone her I must do some reading up on the details of being a bone marrow donor and what it involves. I want to make sure I know exactly what I'm talking about in case she asks me how they do it, and if it hurts and all that kind of thing. I want to be able to give her specific answers and not just fob her off with platitudes.'

'Donating bone marrow doesn't actually hurt but it can have its unpleasant side,' said Adam, quickly adding, 'Or so I've read.'

'Even if she agrees, she may not be a perfect match,' said Petra, sighing deeply, dreading having to speak to the woman. 'Which means we will have gone through all this for nothing…or rather Mrs Gorton will have gone through all this for nothing.'

'Not necessarily,' said Adam. 'Even if she's not a perfect match, if she has brothers or sisters, they might be. Does she have any other children? A half-sibling can often be a good donor.'

'No, I don't think she has any other children,' replied Petra, trying to remember the details of her patient's records.

'Never mind,' said Adam. 'There's always the man's father and his close relatives who can also be tissue-typed in the search for a good match.'

Petra, who'd been making notes of everything Adam said, looked up at him in alarm.

'Oh, Lord, you mean I'm going to have to ask her to reveal the father's name as well? That could be too much for her! She's a nervous wreck as it is. She started having panic attacks when her son attempted to contact her. She'll have a full-blown nervous breakdown if we're not careful!'

'Then let's take it one step at a time,' said Adam calmly. 'Why don't you gently broach the subject with her? Don't, at this stage, say anything about revealing the name of the man's father. If her tissue is a good match it won't be necessary anyway. Once you've convinced her that she could be saving her child's life by being a bone-marrow donor, I'll speak to her about the actual process involved. I know quite a lot about it,' he said, adding quickly, 'I've read up on it recently and can give her the latest information.'

Petra breathed a sigh of relief. 'Thanks, Adam.'

Later that day, before she set out on her calls, Petra managed to find time to check her e-mails. Quite often they were business messages from pharmaceutical companies, hoping to catch her eye and interest her in some new product.

Today she noticed one from Mark and opened it first. It was very short and to the point.

Have to stay in London this weekend. Will phone later. Mark.

'Oh, not again!' She spoke out loud. It was the third weekend in succession that he'd had to stay down there. Petra had really been looking forward to seeing him. It had been ages and…

She had to face it. What was really going through her mind was her need to see Mark in order to re-assure herself about their relationship—and that it wasn't all going horribly wrong. Her feelings hadn't changed towards him…silly of her even to consider the possibility that they had.

It was just that…ever since that evening out with Adam, when she'd let him hold her so close, when she'd almost wanted him to kiss her and…well, it had shaken her quite badly, made her realise that if she and Mark didn't get married very soon, she would constantly be in danger of letting down her guard with Adam. Who knew what might happen next time! No, she decided, I'll agree to buy the very next house Mark takes me round and we'll get mar-ried as quickly as possible. Then she'd be safe. Safe from the temptations of Dr Driscoll!

He seemed to be a most unscrupulous man where women were concerned. Rushing off to Bosnia, de-serting his wife and child…and then coming back and, no doubt stringing her along, promising the woman that it was all going to be fine. Not to men-tion the way he was flirting with Petra when he knew full well she was going to marry another man!

If only he wasn't so charming, so charismatic, so engaging…and, of course, such a good doctor. And if only she could stop thinking about him all the time!

Glancing at her computer screen and Mark's e-mail, she had a good idea. If he couldn't come up north for the weekend, she'd go down to London and stay with him. He'd often mentioned it in the past and she'd never taken him up on the offer. She picked up the phone and dialled his office number. She was put straight through to him.

'Did you get my e-mail?' he asked.

'That's why I'm phoning. I thought I'd come down to London and stay with you. We could go to the theatre and perhaps a concert and—'

'This weekend?' Mark sounded startled.

'That's what we're talking about, isn't it? You said you can't get back home this weekend, so I'm suggesting that I come to see you instead. If Mohammed can't come to the mountain then the mountain will have to come to Mohammed.' She laughed, using one of Mark's favourite phrases.

'This weekend could be a bit of a problem. Can I take a rain check on that?'

'What do you mean, "a bit of a problem"? What kind of problem?' Petra had been expecting Mark to be delighted that she had, at last, offered to come down to London. Instead, he sounded evasive.

'Are you in a meeting?' she asked, wondering if that could be the explanation for his brusque manner.

'No, I'm on my own,' he assured her. 'It's just that I've got some things on this weekend that I can't change and—'

'What kind of things?' She was becoming irked by his excuses. They were always normally so open with one another. Surely he could explain in more convincing detail the reason why he didn't want her around?

'Look,' he said curtly, 'I've got a call on my other line. I must go. Speak to you soon.' He hung up.

Petra was left staring into the phone. Angry tears stung her eyes. It was the first time in all the years she'd known Mark that she'd felt he was lying to her. As she slowly replaced the receiver there was a tap on her door and Adam walked in. She quickly brushed away her tears, smudging her eye make-up in the process.

'Is there anything wrong?' Adam said with concern.

'No,' she said, keeping her voice bright.

'Then why are you crying?'

'Hay fever, I expect. Anyway, what can I do for you, Dr Driscoll?'

It was a strain, putting on a smiling face, but she was determined that she wouldn't give Adam even a hint that there could be anything problematic between herself and Mark.

'I was wondering if you'd managed to get hold of Mrs Gorton,' he said.

'Oh, yes!' Petra was pleased that she had something else to occupy her thoughts at that moment. She would put Mark and his odd behaviour right to the back of her mind and think about it later.

'I spoke to her and arranged to go round and see her this afternoon. I thought it was best to talk about everything…in person, rather than try and explain it over the phone.'

Adam nodded in approval. 'Good idea. Would you like me to come along? I'm due to make a few house calls myself.'

She considered his suggestion for a moment.

'I had planned to speak to her alone first of all.

I've got to at least get her to accept that she is David Smith's mother, for a start. I'm taking along her medical records so I can show her the page where it says she had a baby when she was nineteen.' Petra was in two minds as to whether she would be better approaching that part of the interview alone.

Adam was on the same wavelength.

'I could wait outside in the car,' he suggested. 'If she agrees to be tested as a bone marrow donor you could call me in and I can explain that procedure to her. How does that sound?'

'Sounds great.' She smiled at him with gratitude. She was pleased he'd offered to come with her on the house call. The meeting with Mrs Gorton wasn't going to be easy and she was glad of all the moral support she could get.

Adam was scrutinising her face in a most disconcerting way.

'What's the matter? Have I got spinach on my teeth or something?' she asked.

'No, but you could do a very realistic impression of a panda!'

She'd forgotten she'd smudged her eye make-up when she'd rubbed her eyes. Pulling out a small handbag mirror, she couldn't help bursting out laughing at his very accurate description of how she looked at that precise moment.

'Oh, heavens!' she said, dashing out to the ladies' room to make herself look presentable before she set out on her calls.

Petra and Adam drove in convoy to the leafy suburban road a few miles from the city centre. Petra

parked her car outside a large Victorian villa, Adam
parking his a discreet distance away.

She picked up her doctor's bag and walked over
to Adam.

'I'll come out for you if she agrees to be tested as
a donor. I'll just stand at the door and beckon you
in. OK?'

Adam nodded. 'Good luck.'

As she approached the front door, Petra began to
wish she'd taken an extra degree course in psychol-
ogy! She considered herself to be a reasonably tactful
person...but she was going to be needing a good deal
more than tact to produce a successful outcome to
this particular interview.

Andrea Gorton opened the door to Petra and led
her inside the house and into the sitting room. The
furniture and decorations looked expensive, noted
Petra, but not to the point of ostentation. She was
offered a cup of tea or coffee.

'No, thank you, Mrs Gorton,' she replied.

'I expect you doctors are all very busy,' said
Andrea Gorton, now totally relaxed and almost un-
recognisable from the nervous, agitated woman
who'd presented herself in Petra's surgery a few
weeks previously.

She indicated a plush velvet-covered armchair for
Petra and then seated herself in a matching one a few
feet away.

Petra cast a surreptitious eye round the room.
There were some nice watercolours and oil paintings
on the walls, mostly scenes of the local town and
countryside. There were also several photographs in
silver frames. Many featured Mrs Gorton and a tall,
imposing-looking man whom Petra recognised as be-

ing the local Member of Parliament—Mrs Gorton's husband.

Andrea Gorton saw Petra looking at one of the photographs.

'That was taken last year at the Palace,' she volunteered proudly. 'Buckingham Palace, of course, not the Palace of Westminster! We were at a garden party. That's why I'm wearing that ridiculous hat!'

'And is that…?' Petra pointed to another photograph with a familiar figure standing between Mr and Mrs Gorton.

'Yes, that's the Prime Minister.'

Petra realised that she was playing for time, dreading having to broach the subject of Mrs Gorton's illegitimate son. Closing her eyes for a moment, she gathered her mental strength. She made herself focus on the life-and-death situation that this same son was now facing.

'Mrs Gorton, I made this appointment for a home visit with you for a very special reason.'

'Well, you're very kind to be so concerned about me!' she blithely chatted on. 'But I can assure you that I've had no more of those panic attacks. That's why I didn't get in touch with you to have any tests done. They were really not necessary. Is that why you called on me today? You doctors really are marvellous. I take my hat off to you. Well, I would if I were wearing one!' Andrea Gorton chuckled at her little joke. Petra didn't smile.

'That's not why I'm here, Mrs Gorton.'

'There's nothing the matter, is there?' Her face started to flush as if she was now expecting some bad news. 'You've not discovered something the matter with me, have you?' She added, even more anxiously, 'or with my husband?'

'No, that's not it,' said Petra, picking her words with care. 'It's your son who has something the matter with him.' Petra paused to let this news sink in.

'But I haven't got a son.' Andrea's face had flushed even deeper and the colour was spreading to her neck. 'We haven't got any children. It's one of the sadnesses of our marriage that we were never blessed that way.'

'I'm not talking about you and Mr Gorton,' said Petra quietly.

A pause. A silence. A silence that was broken by a choking sound that escaped from Andrea's orange-painted lips.

A small, irrelevant thought entered Petra's head. It was connected with the unfortunate clash of colours between the deep red of Mrs Gorton's face and the shiny orange of her lipstick. She banished it from her mind.

Reaching into her doctor's bag, she brought out a file. Handing the relevant page to Mrs Gorton, she said gently, 'This was on your records. Can you confirm that it is correct?'

Andrea read it, her eyes riveted to the page. Eventually she nodded.

Petra felt a huge wave of relief that this part of the interview was at least over.

'Why are you here?' Andrea asked sharply. 'Why are you showing me this? It was years ago. My life has changed, I'm a different person now.' She jumped up from her chair and ran out of the room. Petra followed her into the large kitchen.

'I'm sorry to spring this on you, Mrs Gorton, but I have a very good reason for doing so.'

Petra found herself standing behind her patient who was acting in a most extraordinary way, opening and shutting kitchen drawers and cupboards.

'Where the hell is it?' the woman gasped.

'Where's what?' asked Petra, now really worried that the news had pushed her patient into a mental breakdown.

'The paper bag!' shouted Andrea in panic. 'The bloody paper bag!'

She found it and started breathing into it the way Petra had shown her in the surgery.

'Oh,' said Petra in relief. 'You're having a panic attack!'

In a very short time, Andrea's breathing and pulse rate were back to normal.

'You're right,' she said bitterly. 'I did have a baby...nearly thirty years ago. He was illegitimate and my parents made me give him away.'

She turned tortured red eyes on Petra. 'You had to in those days. You young women probably don't understand...but it was different then. Very different.' She pulled out a tissue and blew her nose. 'Girls from "nice" families didn't have babies when they weren't married—it just wasn't done. You had to go and have the baby in another town miles away...that's what I did. And my parents concocted some story about me being moved through my job. And all the time I was waiting, in shame, to have my baby...which I then gave up for adoption. Then I made myself forget about him. I had to. I had to make myself forget about him or I'd have gone mad.'

Petra put a comforting arm around her.

'I understand,' she said.

'I didn't even tell my husband about the baby I'd given away. Ironic really, isn't it? We tried for years to have children and couldn't, and yet when I was a teenager, at a party, I just did it *once* and got pregnant!' She gave a hollow laugh. 'I couldn't even tell you who the father was because I got so drunk at the party I didn't even remember having sex!'

'Well, that cuts off at least one avenue we might have explored,' said Petra as the two women walked back to the sitting room.

'What do you mean—avenue to be explored?'

'Do you remember me saying earlier that your son has something the matter with him?'

'No,' said Andrea. 'Everything went out of my head when I read that note on my record saying, "Male child born in Stoneybridge to Andrea Winterbottom." Perhaps you'd better explain the real reason for your visit today, Doctor.'

Petra waited until they were once again sitting down facing each other in the comfortable armchairs.

'Your son's name is David Smith,' she began. 'He's a research fellow at the university. Sadly, he's been diagnosed with leukaemia—but he has a good chance of a remission, possibly even of a complete remission, if he can get a suitable bone-marrow transplant. He's on a register, searching for a donor, but so far they've had no success in finding him one. His best chance of a good match is through a relative.'

'Oh, I see.'

'That's why he's been trying to contact you, Mrs Gorton. As far as he knows, you are his only blood relative.'

Mrs Gorton had been staring down at her hands

while Petra was speaking. She looked up. Her demeanour was now restored to normal and she spoke calmly.

'Tell me what you want me to do. If I can help him, I will. But I don't want my husband involved in any way. He doesn't have to know, does he?'

'Of course not,' confirmed Petra. 'You could just as easily be a donor for a stranger as for a relative. He doesn't have to ever learn that David Smith is your son. Unless you want to tell him.'

'I don't! And I don't want this to get out. If the press get hold of this story they'll take great delight in using it against my husband. I can see the headlines now! I'm not concerned about my own political career—I'm sick to the teeth with being a city councillor—but my husband's career mustn't suffer because of my foolish behaviour when I was nineteen.'

At this stage, Petra didn't want to get into a discussion about how they could shield her MP husband from bad publicity…she was just so relieved that Andrea had agreed to at least be considered as a donor.

'I'll call in my colleague, Dr Driscoll, to tell you about it. He knows a lot about bone-marrow transplants. He's waiting outside,' said Petra, standing up.

'Dr Driscoll? Is he here, too?'

'He was going on his calls this afternoon and offered to come along and to speak to you if necessary about the procedures involved.'

Petra walked to the front door and beckoned Adam to come in.

When they were all sitting down, he began to explain about acute myeloid leukaemia.

'The treatment for this kind of leukaemia has become so much better in recent years,' he said, 'and the survival rates have increased dramatically. Many patients can be treated very effectively with drugs, but sometimes it's difficult to achieve a cure with drugs alone. And this is what has happened in your son's case.'

He paused to let this information sink in.

'My son!' Andrea said the words almost inaudibly, pressing her hands to her face.

'He needs a bone-marrow transplant. Urgently. He has to find a donor with a matching tissue type, which is an inherited characteristic found in white blood cells. That's why close relatives are often the best source for a good match. Mothers, fathers, brothers, sisters, uncles, aunts…'

'You think I could be a good match?' she asked haltingly.

'Possibly. It would require a simple blood test to check you out. We could take a blood sample today and test it.'

Andrea's eyebrows shot up. 'Today! It's all happening so quickly!'

'I'm afraid it has to happen quickly, Mrs Gorton,' said Adam. 'Without a transplant your son only has a few short years left…five at the most. The sooner he has the transplant, the better his chances will be of a complete remission.'

'I see.'

There was a long pause while Andrea seemed to be weighing up the situation in her mind. She stared at the photographs on the wall. The frown left her face and was replaced by serenity. She gave a deep sigh.

Adam and Petra exchanged a surreptitious glance.

It was beginning to look as if they had persuaded Andrea at least to consider being a donor.

'So,' she said at last. 'It's just a matter of taking a blood sample, is it? Is that all there is to being a donor?'

'A blood sample is all we need initially,' said Adam, 'to test you for a match. But being a bone-marrow donor means just that—it means you have to donate some bone marrow.'

'How? How would I donate marrow?' Andrea addressed the question to both of them but it was Adam who went on to explain.

'It will involve you going into hospital and having a general anaesthetic. A needle will be put into the back of your hip bone and the bone marrow will be drawn out.'

As Adam continued to explain the procedure, Petra noticed that Andrea had gone visibly paler.

'It sounds awful,' she whispered hoarsely.

'It isn't,' responded Adam. 'Trying to save someone's life could never be described as awful. It's a most wonderful feeling, knowing that you might be giving someone the gift of life. You can put up with the slight discomfort involved when you're holding on to that thought.'

'I suppose you doctors are thinking that all the time,' said Andrea, 'that you're saving lives.'

'That's different,' said Adam. 'That's our job. But when you volunteer to be a bone-marrow donor you are actually, physically, giving something of yourself to someone else. You can't get closer to saving a life than that. If you saw someone drowning in a river—you'd want to jump in and try to save them. It's a bit like that, really…it's life-saving and life-giving at the same time.'

Petra felt herself incredibly moved by Adam's words. She realised he was doing his utmost to persuade Andrea to take the plunge and agree to be a donor…but something in his expression made her believe that he wasn't just speaking as a doctor to a patient, he was speaking from the heart.

It was clear that Andrea was also very moved.

'What if my blood test shows that I'm not a good match? What then?'

'Then your son will have to keep on hoping that he finds a match on the register before too long…before too late.'

'Then we've no time to lose.' Andrea rolled up her sleeve and held out her arm. 'Please, take the blood sample now…and get back to me with the results as soon as possible.'

CHAPTER SIX

THE London train arrived in Milchester station within a minute of its due time. Petra knew this because the guard announced it as the carriages pulled alongside the platform.

Normally she wouldn't have noted such an inconsequential occurrence…but tonight was different. She found herself noticing even the tiniest detail—for instance, the colour of the buttons on the mobile phone used by the man sitting next to her throughout the three-hour train journey.

She didn't feel irritated by his behaviour. In fact, she didn't feel anything. She hadn't felt anything for at least five hours. Ever since she'd discovered Mark's treachery. Perhaps it was nature's way of protecting you against bad news, she said to herself as she stepped down from the train and walked the short distance to the station car park when she'd left her car that morning.

She drove in a trance through town to the small private car park belonging to the town houses. As she turned off the ignition all the pent-up emotion hit her with a frightening force and, clutching the steering-wheel, she began to sob her heart out.

There was a knock on the car window. The light in the car park was good but her windows were now so steamed up she wasn't able to see clearly out of them. She could just make out the face of a man peering in at her. She gave a small, involuntary scream as her hand flew to her mouth. Was she about to be mugged?

'It's only me,' said a familiar voice. 'Is that you, Petra?'

Breathing a sigh of relief, she wound down her window a couple of inches.

'I thought you were a robber!' she said. Winding it down a little further, she found herself looking straight at Adam Driscoll. He was bending so that his face was level with hers.

'I'm so glad to see you!' she burst out, unable to help the flood of tears that starting pouring down her face once again.

'Open the passenger door,' he said, before walking round and sliding into the seat next to hers.

'Tell me what's the matter,' he said. 'Has something terrible happened?'

He slid his arm around her shoulder and pulled her to him. At first she found she was unable to speak and tell him why she was crying. All she could do was sob uncontrollably, her tears soaking through his shirt.

He let her cry, stroking her hair and uttering soothing words.

Eventually, by a combination of Adam's comforting presence and her own will-power, she managed to stop crying. She took from her bag a handful of tissues and mopped up her tears and blew her nose.

'Crying's not very glamorous,' she said, catching a glimpse of herself in the car mirror. 'Not like in the movies,' she sniffed.

'So, what's all this about?' Adam cupped her face in his hand. 'This is the second time in as many weeks that I've caught you crying. And don't fob me off with that old hayfever story. You'd been crying then and you're certainly crying now.'

She took a deep breath.

'It's Mark,' she said. 'He's having an affair!' As she spoke the words her bottom lip began to tremble.

Adam hugged her to him.

'Oh, is that all?' he said with huge relief. 'I was dreading you saying it was some illness or disease you'd discovered you'd got! Thank goodness it's only your engagement.'

That stung her into action. Pulling back from him, she said fiercely, '*Only* my engagement? A man I've known nearly all my life, known and trusted and loved—and now I find out he's having an affair!'

'People do, you know…have affairs. At least be glad you found out before you got married.' Adam kept his arm round her and the two of them looked straight ahead at the misted-over windscreen. Eventually Petra spoke.

'Yes, you're right,' she said quietly. 'If I'm honest with myself, I should have seen it coming. All that time he was spending in London! I might have known it wasn't all connected with work. Anyway, today I decided to surprise him by turning up unexpectedly on his doorstep…but the only person I surprised was myself.'

'What happened? Can you bear to talk about it?' Adam's voice was gentle and comforting.

She took a deep breath.

'Well, as I told you, I'd decided that if he couldn't find the time to come up to Milchester I would go down to London. He keeps asking me to do just that.' She checked herself. 'He *used* to ask me. That was before…before all this.' She bit her lip to stop herself from crying again.

Adam's grip tightened on her shoulder. She continued.

'I took a cab round to the building where his company flat is and rang the bell. It's one of those where you have to wait for the person inside to press the security button to let you into the lobby area—you know the sort.'

Adam nodded.

'It hadn't occurred to me that Mark might not be in, midmorning on a Saturday. I know he said he had a lot on that weekend and that's why he couldn't come up here. But I just thought he meant he'd taken a lot of work home with him. Anyway, I waited outside for ages and it was quite obvious that he wasn't in. I thought that if I could wait in the lobby, perhaps I'd see him when he did come in. So I pressed the bell of another flat, one that I thought was near his.'

She took another deep breath.

'A man answered and I explained who I was and that could he, please, let me into the building so I could wait for Mark. The man sounded very suspicious and obviously thought I was just trying to get into the building—to rob them all, I suppose!'

She gave a nervous laugh at the memory.

'So what happened?'

'He said he was coming down and would talk to me. So I waited outside and after about five minutes the man let me in. I told him again that I was Mark's fiancée and that I'd just like to wait for him inside. "He's not here," he said. "Well, I know that," I said. "That's why I had to ring your bell. Look," I said, "I'm not a burglar, you know, I'm going to marry him.'' And I flashed my engagement ring at him. The man then went from being very suspicious of me to being rather embarrassed. ''He's not here for the whole weekend,'' he said. ''Mark's gone away to Newmarket. Didn't he tell you? He asked me to keep an eye on his flat.'''

'Newmarket! Why Newmarket?' said Adam.

'That's just what I said.' Petra shuddered at the humiliation she'd felt when it had become obvious to Mark's neighbour that he'd kept his fiancée in the dark.

'Apparently Mark had gone away the previous evening...for a dirty weekend in Newmarket!'

'Is that what the man said?'

'No, he just looked pityingly at me when he told me that they'd left on Friday evening. ''They?'' I said. ''Yes, Mark and the young lady. I believe she's a colleague,'' he added quickly, thinking that would make things sound better.'

'Perhaps you're jumping to the wrong conclusion,' said Adam quietly.

'I'm sure I'm not!' retorted Petra. 'It all fits into place now. That's the reason Mark's been so keen to spend time in London—or rather *she's* the reason! And no wonder he didn't want me coming down this weekend when I suggested it a few days ago. I just thought he was bogged down with work when all along he was planning to go to Newmarket with his paramour! He lied to me!'

Adam touched her left hand and in the dark sought out her third finger.

'What did you do with your ring?'

'I put it in an envelope with a cryptic note and stuck it in his letterbox to await his return. I certainly didn't want to wear it for a moment longer.' She sniffed and wiped away another tear. 'The silly thing is, I just can't stop crying.'

'Broken romances are sad occasions,' he said. 'From the sound of it he played a big role in your life. It's not something you can forget in a few hours.'

'He did.' Petra nodded. 'He played a really big role, for years.'

'How did you meet him?'

'It was when I was a little girl,' recalled Petra. 'My father was an army doctor and he was posted abroad for quite a few years. I loved living in all the different countries but found it very hard to make any permanent friends as we moved so often. When I was seven my parents decided that I should go away to boarding school in England. I was a boarder for three years until my father retired from the army. They were the most miserable three years of my life!' She shivered as she remembered the loneliness of those early days when she'd been consumed with homesickness.

'You poor lamb,' said Adam, hugging her close to him.

'When my dad retired he bought a share in a country practice in Cheshire and I was able to leave boarding school and live at home again. That's when I met Mark. I was a very shy and withdrawn only child and Mark, who was a year older and also an only child, became the big brother I'd always wanted. He included me in all his games and became the first real friend I'd ever had. I hero-worshipped him. Sorry, Adam,' she said, snivelling into her handkerchief again, 'it's all very painful to me.'

Speaking about those early days had brought it all back to her—how Mark, always an attention-seeker, had loved the way Petra had idolised and adored him, following him around, obeying his commands like a willing slave.

'And I suppose hero-worship turned into love.' There was no sarcasm in Adam's voice as he made this statement.

'That's right. Our engagement came as no surprise to anyone. Both families were delighted and it was as if everyone who'd ever known us had also taken it for granted that one day Petra Phillips would marry Mark Campbell. Until today. That's it...all over. *Finito.*'

'It's good that you found out now, and not when it was too late,' he said, repeating his earlier sentiments. 'Finding out that you're not compatible after you've married is a whole lot worse.'

They sat in silence for a while. She began to draw strength from him and also began to dwell on what he'd said, and what, if anything, he was hinting at indirectly. Was he perhaps implying that he had been married and had then discovered that he and his wife had been incompatible?

'You seem to know a lot about broken romances. Perhaps you're speaking from experience?' she ventured.

'I've certainly been there,' he confirmed. 'But a broken heart mends very quickly once you realise it was the wrong person. At the time it hurts like hell, and you just want to escape from all that pain. I even considered joining the Foreign Legion!'

'Honestly?'

'Nearly honestly. I signed on for Bosnia instead!'

Petra looked up at him.

'Is that why you went to Bosnia? Because of a woman?'

'Mainly,' said Adam. 'But who knows? I might have gone anyway. And once there, helping to deal with the victims of war, it certainly put things in perspective and stopped me feeling sorry for myself.'

'Are you suggesting that's what I'm doing—feeling sorry for myself?'

'I suppose you're entitled to do that, but not for too long. I could see a lot wrong with that relationship even from the small bit of it I saw.'

'That's extremely presumptuous of you!' Petra was quickly regaining her fighting spirit. 'I'd say you knew nothing about our relationship!'

'It's true I didn't know much about it…but I do know something. I do know he didn't kiss you like this…'

Before she could reply, his lips came down on hers. At first she stiffened and pulled away from him, but he was insistent and held her firmly in his grasp until she found she was captivated by his touch. Her body seemed boneless and she leaned into his embrace. Slowly, tantalisingly, he deepened his kiss, opening her lips and quickening her pulse. She'd never wanted a man's kiss as much as she wanted this… Every touch, every caress made her tremble. The heat burned under her skin as she responded to him like a feral animal.

It wasn't until she felt his hand move to her breast that she pulled back in alarm. What on earth was she doing? One minute she was heartbroken, the next she was deeply snogging another man…only hours after she'd given the engagement ring back!

'You're taking advantage of me,' she said, feeling guilty for her reckless behaviour.

'Of course I am,' said Adam, giving a deep throaty laugh. 'And we both enjoyed every second of it!'

'We've got to stop this right now,' she said, rummaging about for her handbag.

'Have I made you cross?' asked Adam, sounding not in the least concerned as he continued to smile at her.

'Yes, you have. I'm really quite cross now,' she said, not daring to look him in the eye for fear of bursting out laughing.

'Good,' he said. 'Because I'd rather have you cross than crying.'

They got out of Petra's car and began to walk the short distance home.

'Oh, by the way,' said Adam. 'I've got some good news about Mrs Gorton's blood test. Against great odds, it's an almost perfect match.'

On Monday morning, Mark tried to phone her. She'd left strict instructions with the receptionist that he wasn't to be put through. Meanwhile, she managed to put all thoughts of him to the back of her mind by keeping herself constantly occupied, throwing herself into her work with grim determination.

Hannah had phoned in sick and Petra immediately volunteered to take on her colleague's shifts and clinics. By the end of day she was so exhausted she could barely drag herself home to bed. When she walked in through her front door she could see the light flashing on her answering machine.

'Six messages,' she noted aloud, 'and I bet they're all from that lying Mark!'

She waited until she was sitting down with a mug of coffee in her hands before deciding to listen to them. 'It's no use,' she said to the phone, before pressing the replay button, 'I'm not going to listen to your pathetic excuses! And as for having you back, that is definitely not on the cards!'

But she did. And it was.

On Tuesday morning, Petra walked jauntily into Adam's room. He was pleased to see that she was looking bright-eyed and perky. Obviously coping well with the broken engagement. Not a hint of the utter distress he'd come across in the car park on Saturday.

'I've something to tell you,' she said, sliding into the chair opposite him. 'It was all a terrible misunderstanding.'

'What was?'

'Mark taking that woman to Newmarket.'

Adam leaned back in his chair. He felt as if the ground were giving way beneath him. 'You mean your former boyfriend told you a pack of convincing lies?'

Petra laughed gaily. Her happy spirit contrasted with a heaviness of heart that had suddenly descended on him.

'Apparently he went to Newmarket to see a client who's a horse trainer—and the work colleague he went with is actually the daughter of this client. She doesn't want to handle family business—for obvious reasons—but she needed to go along to explain things to Mark. It was as simple as that!'

'But I thought you said he'd lied to you. I thought

he'd told you that he was going to be in London all
weekend?'

'I think I presumed that he was,' said Petra. 'He
did say he was working all weekend, which was true.
He just omitted to tell me he was working in
Newmarket.'

'So,' said Adam, a slight bitterness creeping into
his voice, 'the engagement's back on again, is it?'

'Yep. He's coming up next weekend and will
bring the ring with him. Just thought I'd put you in
the picture as you were so wonderful when I believed
everything had gone pear-shaped. You're a real pal,
Adam. A true friend in need.' She blew him a kiss
and then walked out of his room.

'A true friend,' muttered Adam. 'Huh!'

At the next practice meeting Hannah, who'd returned
to work the previous day, was sitting next to Petra.
She noticed a large bruise on the side of Hannah's
head and asked about it.

'Bumped into a stone pillar when I was bell-
ringing,' she replied, making an unsuccessful attempt
to cover the bruised area with her hair.

On hearing this explanation, Adam said, 'I didn't
think bell-ringing was such a dangerous hobby!'

'Hardly dangerous,' replied Hannah lightly.

'But that's quite a big bruise you have there,' he
said.

'It's no big deal. I'll make a better attempt at con-
cealing it tomorrow with a bit of make-up.'

'What about those other bruises?' Adam asked.

'Which ones?' she said defensively.

'The bruises on your arms and legs. I noticed them
earlier. Have you had a fall or anything?'

'No,' she replied quickly. 'Just bell-ringing! And don't look at me like that, you two! It's not a dangerous hobby if you watch where you're walking and avoid stone pillars.'

'You are a one!' said Petra. 'I never even knew you *were* a bell-ringer. Tell me more.' Petra leaned closer to her colleague. 'I bet there's a man involved!'

'How did you guess?' She spoke in a conspiratorial tone, lowering her voice. 'Keep it under your hat, but I've met this gorgeous new man. He's a bell-ringer at our local church. He's not as dishy as Adam—most men aren't—but he's pretty good-looking for an older man!'

'I'm very pleased for you,' said Petra. Hannah didn't appear to have had many men in her life. She'd once confided that she'd been married some years ago to 'an absolute rotter' and Petra presumed she was now either divorced or separated. Hannah gave the impression it had all happened a long time ago, possibly fifteen or twenty years previously.

'I say, isn't it good news about that leukaemia patient of yours, the one who needs a bone-marrow transplant,' said Hannah to Adam, abruptly changing the subject.

'It is so far. But he has a long way to go before he's out of the woods,' replied Adam, striking a note of caution. 'If the bone marrow doesn't take successfully the first time, he may need another attempt. However, things are looking good, with Mrs Gorton's tissue type being such a good match.'

The practice meeting then got under way, and no more comments were made about Hannah's bruises or her new boyfriend. At the end of the meeting everyone left for their own rooms and Petra was surprised when Adam followed her into her room and shut the door.

'There was something I wanted to speak to you about,' he announced in a conspiratorial voice. 'Did you believe all that stuff about bell-ringing?'

Petra wrinkled her brow in puzzlement. 'Why not?'

'I think maybe Hannah's hiding something. All that bruising…it could be an indication of a bleeding disorder, purpura.'

'I hadn't thought about that,' said Petra. 'Purpura can be a sign of so many diseases or even caused by drugs she may be taking at the minute. When she was off sick earlier in the week she didn't really say what was wrong with her, did she? And I didn't ask her…it just never occurred to me that she might be hiding some serious illness.'

'I could be overreacting,' admitted Adam. 'I thought I'd get your opinion about the bell-ringing story. Did it sound genuine to you?'

'Yes, I think it did. She told me, out of earshot of the others, that she's got a new man in her life. She met him through bell-ringing. So…'

'Enough said.' Adam laughed. 'I believe her story. But, as I said to Hannah, I'd no idea it was so dangerous!'

'It can be. Haven't you heard those stories about bell-ringers who forget to let go of the rope and are pulled up into the bell tower?' Petra put on her wide-eyed, scared look. 'The bells! The bells!'

'That's a different story!' Adam laughed again. 'That's *The Hunchback of Notre Dame!*'

Petra smiled at him, glad he'd come in. He always

had this effect on her, lifting her spirits, making her feel good. And she'd not forgotten how grateful she was to him for being there and comforting her when she'd thought the worst of Mark. He really was a wonderful man. Adam that was, not Mark. But, of course, Mark was wonderful, too, in a different kind of way.

Two days later, Petra drove into the medical centre car park and into her usual parking space.

She was locking her car door when Adam and Hannah pulled in and parked their cars close to hers. All three colleagues walked into the medical centre together.

'You're very optimistic,' Petra said to Hannah, referring to her sunglasses. 'It looks so dull today I think we could be in for a storm, not sunny weather.'

'I'd take them off now,' said Adam, joining in the conversation, 'or you could end up bumping into the door. It's like night out here!'

Hannah fingered her dark glasses but didn't remove them.

'I think I'd better keep them on. I've got a couple of shiners.'

Adam peered behind her glasses and exclaimed, 'Where did you get those?' He pulled her glasses a little way down the bridge of her nose, revealing two extremely painful-looking black eyes. 'You look as if you've gone ten rounds with a prizefighter!'

Petra was also shocked at her colleague's appearance.

'Good gracious, Hannah, you look terrible! Who did that do you?'

Hannah stayed silent for a moment before covering her eyes once more with her dark glasses.

'No one,' she said, giving a small laugh. 'I tripped going up the stairs at home. Banged myself right on the face.'

'I thought it might have been something to do with bell-ringing,' said Petra as the three of them walked into the medical centre.

'Why ever should you think that?' asked Hannah lightly.

'Because that's what happened last time,' replied Petra. 'You know, when you walked into those stone pillars.'

'Oh, yes, I remember,' said Hannah. 'No, this was at home. I just tripped up, as you do.'

'Better take more water with it next time!' said Adam.

'I hadn't been drinking if that's what you were thinking.' Hannah sounded quite upset by the suggestion.

'Only joking, Hannah,' said Adam. 'Only joking.'

CHAPTER SEVEN

AMONG the mail in Petra's in-tray was a handwritten envelope without a stamp. She recognised the spidery writing as being that of her senior partner, Don Michaels.

On opening the envelope, she saw it was a printed invitation to Don's and Val's silver wedding celebration in ten days' time. Her name—and Mark's—had been written on the invitation card. She checked her diary and found that she was able to go, but she was almost certain that Mark would be down in London on that date and she'd have to accept the invitation for herself only.

In the weeks since their engagement had been back on, Mark had appeared to be making a great effort to spend a lot more time in the Milchester office. They saw each other nearly every day and they were beginning to make definite plans for their wedding, now fixed tentatively for six months' time.

Mark had dropped his insistence that they buy a house first. And in return Petra had agreed to consider moving to London. In the meantime, they would live at her small town house.

'We may as well live here, instead of trying to find somewhere to rent,' Petra had suggested. To her surprise Mark had agreed. He seemed to be agreeing to everything at the moment. Ever since the misunderstanding about the Newmarket weekend, he'd changed, Petra had noticed, in very subtle ways. He

wasn't as forceful and demanding as before. His eyes
had a far-away look, as if his mind was preoccupied
with other matters. And he'd lost weight. Nothing to
get worried about, but nevertheless Petra was concerned.

'Are you eating enough?' she'd ask him.

'You sound like my mother,' Mark would joke.

'I think you're working too hard.'

'Probably. But it's only for a short time, until I
get my career sorted out.'

Petra couldn't help wondering if it was another of
Mark's ploys to get his own way. It seemed to be
working! Against her better judgement she had said
she was prepared to live and work in London. She
hadn't mentioned anything to her partners yet, but
the time was drawing close when she was going to
have to say something. It was only fair to give them
as much notice as possible so that they could find a
replacement.

Picking up the invitation, she scribbled in the
words 'Don & Val's party' in her diary, wrote a
quick note accepting the invitation and popped it in
her out-tray.

'Twenty-five years married!' she said out loud in
a voice that combined admiration and misgiving. A
small voice in the back of her head said, Will you
and Mark make it that far?

'Yes, of course we will,' she said, to no one in
particular.

Don and Val Michaels lived in a modern bungalow
with a large garden in a leafy suburb a few miles
from the centre of Milchester.

A marquee had been erected on the back lawn and

the hundred or so guests were standing or sitting inside it or were outside in the garden, enjoying the last rays of the sun on the warm summer evening.

Petra had accepted a lift from Adam who'd offered to take her when he'd learned that Mark hadn't been able to come.

'No sense in us both driving, is there?' said Adam, who had in recent weeks had appeared to have got the message that Petra was off limits as far as flirting was concerned. Once Adam had learned that her engagement was definitely on, he'd seemed to be keeping out of her way—no bumping into each other 'accidentally on purpose' and certainly no deep, fiery kisses! Petra still blushed at the memory of their kiss in her car when she'd believed Mark had been cheating on her.

As they arrived at the party they were greeted by their hosts. Don was wearing a sparkly silver shirt in honour of the occasion and Val, a statuesque, handsome woman, was in a lemon silk dress and sported a dazzling blue and yellow silk scarf.

'How nice that you could both come,' Val effused. 'I'm only sorry that your young man couldn't make it, Petra. I was so looking forward to meeting him.'

'Mark had to go to an important meeting in London, I'm afraid.'

'And isn't it a pity about Hannah having to cry off?' remarked Val.

'I didn't know she had,' Petra replied, surprised by the news. Earlier that day at the surgery Hannah had promised them a glimpse of the new boyfriend whom she was supposedly bringing along to the party.

'She phoned about half an hour ago,' Don told

them. 'Said she felt unwell. And I must say she didn't sound her usual self at all. Quite down and low-spirited.'

Petra and Adam exchanged glances. Then, clutching a glass of sparkling white wine, Petra strolled into the garden.

Adam joined her a few minutes later. 'Do you know anyone here?' he asked, casting his eyes around the other guests, searching for a familiar face. 'Ah. I've just spotted Robin and Patrick,' he said. 'Unless you want a lecture on how tough it is making ends meet, I suggest we walk in a different direction. They're great doctors but even greater bores.'

'That's a little unfair,' said Petra, only half in agreement. 'Patrick's not too bad these days now that his divorce is finally through. And it did sound as if his former wife took him to the cleaners, so he probably had good reason to grumble.'

'You've only heard one side of the story, remember,' said Adam.

'That's true.'

'Always a bad mistake, jumping to conclusions too soon.'

'Are you referring to anything or anyone in particular?' she said, knowing only too well what Adam was alluding to. It was obvious that he meant the way she had presumed that Mark had been having an affair when he'd only gone away on business. She felt her skin prickle.

Adam grinned. 'No. I wasn't referring to anything or anyone in particular. By the way,' he said, pausing to take a drink, 'have you any idea what's running in the one-thirty at Newmarket?'

Before she could formulate a reply a waitress with

a tray of finger food appeared at her elbow. She took the opportunity to change the subject.

'Is that Patrick's new woman with him, do you think?'

'I expect so,' said Adam, glancing in the direction of their partner. 'Patrick told me he'd met this ravishing redhead and was madly in love with her.'

'Wasn't his first wife a ravishing redhead?'

'I believe so. Looks as if he could be heading for trouble again!'

Although Petra could tell that Adam was only joking, she didn't want to let his sweeping remark go unchallenged.

'Poor Patrick,' she said. 'Are you saying he shouldn't go out with a redhead again in case he repeats his mistakes?'

'Not at all! I admire the man for his bravery. For being a risk-taker.' Adam's eyes danced mischievously. He was enjoying winding her up.

'And I suppose you're a risk-taker?'

'Most certainly. It's the only way to be. The only way to live a fulfilled life.'

There was something in his tone of voice that made Petra take his remark personally. 'Are you saying that I'm not a risk taker?'

Adam didn't answer straight away. When he did he gazed deep into her eyes as if he was trying to look into her soul.

'That's right. I'm not talking professionally, of course. And I don't know if you're the kind of person who does parachute jumps for charity. But I'd say you aren't someone who takes risks as far as your emotional life is concerned.'

'Oh!' she said, reeling away from him, shocked by his directness.

He grabbed her arm, thinking that she might be about to fall over.

'Excuse my bluntness, but you did ask,' he said.

She shook his arm from hers. 'You know nothing about it! You know nothing about me and Mark…because I'm sure that's what you're getting at!' She could feel the colour rising in her cheeks.

'You'd be surprised,' he said. 'I know quite a lot about you and Mark. I don't have to be a psychologist to work out that little number.'

'What?'

'How you and he were children together. How he was the dependable big brother figure that you hero-worshipped. How both families took it for granted that you and he were just perfect for one another. It all sounds a bit dull and predictable, don't you think? Doesn't leave much room for excitement or spontaneity—'

'Mark is *wonderful*,' interrupted Petra furiously. 'He's kind and strong…and, yes, so he's a bit predictable. There's nothing wrong with that. Mark knows exactly what he wants from life.'

'I dare say,' said Adam. 'But what about you? What do *you* want from life? Do you want a dull, predictable marriage to a dull, predictable man? Sounds to me as if you're marrying Mark because he's always been there, like a safety net. It's good to have a safety net, don't get me wrong. I'd like one myself. But I don't know if I'd want to marry one!'

Petra took a deep breath. She was determined not to let Adam make her lose her temper. She was, she told herself, at a party after a hard week's work, and she was supposed to be enjoying herself!

She lifted her voice to make it sound light and casual. 'Are you saying that if I marry Mark I could be heading for trouble, like Patrick and his glamorous new redhead?'

'Trouble's no problem.' Adam laughed, a trifle harshly. 'Trouble I can take. It's regret I can't take.'

'Regret? You think I'll regret marrying Mark?'

'Who knows? More importantly, you might regret *not* marrying someone else.'

There was an embarrassing silence between them.

'If you'll excuse me,' she muttered, 'I think I've got an eyelash in my eye. I'll just find the bathroom and remove it.'

Petra dashed back into the house.

When the meal was announced, Petra was glad to note that there was a table plan and that she was seated at the other end of the marquee from Adam. One deep conversation with him about her personal life was plenty for one evening. She was glad of the opportunity to find herself with people who knew nothing about Mark and therefore couldn't make any judgmental comments about her engagement.

Driving home with Adam after the party, Petra was relieved that he didn't broach the subject again. He probably realised he'd gone too far, she mused. Instead, Adam turned on the radio and they drove along in companionable silence.

A few drops of rain had fallen as they were leaving the party and within minutes the few drops had turned into a deluge. The wipers, working overtime, could just about cope with the downpour. They drove slowly until the rain eased off and they could put on a bit more speed. They were only a short distance from home when they ran into a traffic jam.

It was at a point where the main Milchester road went over an old canal. About a dozen cars were lined up behind a large vehicle with a flashing yellow light.

'Damn,' said Adam, braking and bringing the car to a halt. 'Looks as if there's been an accident.'

At that moment an ambulance, its blue light flashing, went past them in the opposite direction.

Adam switched off the engine and reached into the back seat for his golf umbrella. By now the rain had become a persistent drizzle.

'I'll go and see if anyone needs help,' he said. 'You stay here for a moment.

As Petra waited for Adam to return she could hear the sound of machinery. She wound down the window to hear it better and to try and work out what it was. To her surprise she realised that the large vehicle with the flashing light was some sort of mobile crane and it was in the process of pulling something from the canal.

A bright searchlight was focused on the operation. As she watched she saw a car emerging from the canal's murky depth, and as it was winched up, gallons of water poured from its opened doors.

After a few minutes she saw Adam walking back along the line of traffic. He shook the rain from the umbrella and put it in the boot before getting back into the car. He had a grim expression on his face.

'What's going on?'

'A car veered off the road, hit a lamppost and top-

pled over the bridge into the water. No other vehicle
was involved but someone saw what happened and
called the emergency services. The driver was pulled
out of the car and taken away by ambulance.'

'That must have been the ambulance we saw as
we arrived,' said Petra. 'The driver, was he all right?'

Adam shook his head. 'I don't think so. I spoke
to a policeman who saw the body—well, the person,
taken out of the water. He wasn't even sure if the
driver was a man or a woman. He didn't get a good
view before the paramedics took over.'

Adam stared ahead. Petra felt there was something
else he needed to say.

'What is it?' she asked. 'What's the problem?'

'The car. The one they pulled out of the water. I
recognised the number plate.'

Petra went cold.

'Whose car was it?'

'Hannah's. Hannah Hughes. It was her car.'

Twelve minutes. Twelve and a half minutes. Thirteen
minutes. Petra gritted her teeth and counted the seconds.

They were still stuck in the traffic jam on the
bridge over the canal, unable to move the car in either direction. She was staring at the digital clock on
the dashboard in an effort to take her mind off the
dreadful revelation that it had been Hannah's car
they'd pulled out of the water in front of their eyes.

'Try phoning her again,' said Adam.

'It's no use. There's no reply. But I'll try again if
you think I should.' Petra pressed the redial button
on her mobile. It rang out as before, unanswered.

The traffic started to move, directed by the police.

'What should we do?' asked Petra. 'Go round to Hannah's, just in case? Or go straight to Milchester General, if that's where the ambulance was going?'

'Let's do both,' suggested Adam. 'We'll go to the hospital after we've called round at Hannah's house. You never know. It could be good news... Someone could have stolen her car, which means it couldn't have been her driving it.'

'In that case...' began Petra, but she left the sentence unfinished. In that case, why didn't Hannah answer her phone?

They drove through the centre of town and out towards the suburban village where Hannah lived. Her small house, the last one in a row of former mill workers' cottages, had roses round the door and hollyhocks growing in the tiny front garden.

Parking his car outside, Adam switched off the engine and they sat in silence for a few moments, surveying the scene.

The house was in complete darkness.

'She could be upstairs in bed,' said Petra, not really believing it herself.

Adam looked up at the first-floor windows. 'Wouldn't she pull down the blinds or draw the curtains if she was going to bed?'

'Looks pretty deserted, doesn't it?' said Petra, hope fading fast.

'I'll go and check, just in case,' he said, opening the glove compartment and taking out a torch. 'You might as well stay here.'

She nodded glumly.

He shone the torch in front of him as he walked the short distance to the house and then turned the beam on the window, pointing it into every corner of the front room. The beam flickered around eerily, making Adam look suspiciously like a burglar sizing up a house for a prospective break-in. After he'd illuminated every section of the room, he did it again, this time more slowly and thoroughly, holding the light on a particular spot.

'Come here, Petra,' he called, beckoning her to join him. 'Come here a minute.'

She leapt out of the car and rushed to his side.

'What is it?'

'I can just make out a strange shape in the corner, behind the armchair. What do you think it is?'

Petra peered in at the spot where Adam was shining his torch. It wasn't a very powerful beam and didn't light up the whole of the room. But it was bright enough to show something a little odd lying on the floor. A roll of carpet? A couple of bin bags?

She tapped on the window and then banged more loudly. 'Hannah,' she called out, more in hope than expectation. A roll of carpet was hardly going to answer back.

Adam also banged on the window while keeping the beam focused on the object on the floor.

'I think I saw it move!'

There was definitely a movement and they both saw it.

'She's in there!' said Adam.

Petra put a restraining hand on him. 'Somebody's in there. It may not be Hannah.'

They ran to the front door which was firmly closed. Even Adam's weight against it couldn't made it budge. Petra went round to the back and made a startling discovery.

'Adam! The back door's open!'

They entered the house cautiously, switching on lights as they went along. Their eyes were drawn to the stone kitchen floor and a trail of blood that led out of the kitchen into the hallway and through the open door of the living room.

The trail became a pool and lying in it was the prone body of their medical partner. Her eyes were open and for a moment they thought she was dead. Then she blinked in the bright light of the torch and Petra gasped with relief.

'Oh, Hannah! You're alive!'

Without a word being said, they swung into action, working as a team with smooth efficiency. While Adam went to Hannah, Petra phoned for an ambulance and then joined him at Hannah's side.

There was so much blood, bright crimson against the pale gold of the carpet. Their shoes squelched in it and it soaked through their clothes as they knelt by the side of the injured woman.

Adam cradled Hannah's head in his arm and shook her gently, trying to prevent her from slipping back into unconsciousness.

'Can you hear me, Hannah?' he asked. 'She's breathing,' he told Petra, 'but it's very shallow. And her pulse is weak. Not surprising when you see how much blood she's lost.'

'Where's the cut?'

'Some blood's coming from her nose,' said Adam. 'But that seems to be stopping. I think most of the blood is from a wound at the back of her head. I've raised her head up slightly and pressed it against my arm to try and control that area of bleeding. Just have another check around, Petra, and see if you can find any other place where she might be losing blood.'

The injured woman gave a groan and opened her eyes again.

'Hannah,' said Petra close to her ear, 'It's Mark and Petra. We're here to help you. We'll soon have you safe and well. Can you hear me? Squeeze my hand if you can.'

To her relief and delight Petra felt a small amount of pressure from the hand she was holding in hers. Then Hannah tried to speak.

'Phone,' she said.

'Don't worry, we've phoned for an ambulance.'

'Heard the phone,' said Hannah. 'Woke me up. Couldn't get to it.'

'That was us,' said Petra. 'We tried your number a short time ago.'

'Jack went.'

'Who's Jack, Hannah?' Adam asked.

'Bell-ringer.'

'Jack's the name of her bell-ringing boyfriend,' Petra told Adam. 'He must have been here earlier. They were supposed to be coming to Don and Val's party, remember?' Speaking gently to Hannah, she asked, 'Did Jack do this to you?'

'Yes. Drunken bastard.'

'He's not here any more, don't worry about that,' said Adam reassuringly.

'Heard him drive away,' said Hannah. 'Tell the police. Catch him. Lock him up.'

'I think the police know where he is,' said Adam. 'He's out of harm's way.' Petra and Adam glanced at each other in mutual understanding.

Outside they saw the flashing blue light of the ambulance and heard the paramedics jumping out of their vehicle. Petra went to the front door to let them in.

CHAPTER EIGHT

BY THE beginning of the next week things had settled down somewhat. Hannah was making good progress in Milchester General after a massive blood transfusion, and a new locum called Helen had come in at very short notice and taken over her patients.

'The man driving her car, was he that bell-ringer?' asked Patrick at the practice meeting.

'Yes,' Adam replied.

'Dead on arrival, wasn't he?' said Robin

'I believe so.'

'"Never send to know for whom the bell tolls; it tolls for *thee*!"' said Robin in a theatrical voice. He nudged Patrick who tried, unsuccessfully, to suppress a giggle.

'That's not hugely funny,' said Adam, 'considering the tragic circumstances. We've got a partner who nearly died after a severe beating and a drunk driver who did die. Without sounding too pompous, I'd say it was hardly cause for laughter.'

'Let's go on, shall we?' said Don, calling the meeting to order.

Twenty minutes into Petra's morning surgery, Andrea Gorton walked into the room and sat down.

'What can I do for you, Mrs Gorton?' asked Petra, her fingers crossed under her desk. She was desperately hoping that the woman hadn't changed her mind about being a bone-marrow donor.

'I'm going into hospital tomorrow, as you know,' she said, 'for this bone-marrow thing.'

'Everything all right, I presume?'

'Medically speaking, everything's fine.' The woman was looking as agitated as when she'd been experiencing the panic attacks some weeks back.

'It's quite understandable that you should feel nervous about the procedure,' said Petra. 'Would you like to speak again to Dr Driscoll? He's very up to date on what you can expect to happen.'

Andrea shook her head emphatically. 'That's not what's troubling me. I've never shied away from that kind of thing—discomfort, even pain.' She looked down at her hands, clasping them tightly together to stop them from shaking.

'I've always been very reticent about my private life,' she said, not looking Petra in the eye. 'We, my husband and I, have to be very careful to avoid any kind of scandal or gossip. I am a city councillor but, more importantly, my husband is the local Member of Parliament. This is just the kind of story that the tabloids would sell their grandmothers for. I can just see the headline now. MP's Wife Is Unmarried Mother!'

'Things have changed, Mrs Gorton…times have changed. Having an illegitimate baby is nothing these days. You said so yourself.'

At the mention of the word 'illegitimate' Andrea flinched as if she'd been struck.

'Things haven't changed that much,' she said. 'It's still open season on the lives of people in the public eye. My poor husband would be hauled up in front of the party hierarchy to explain it all away—and then he'd have to face it all again at a Milchester

North constituency meeting. ''You didn't tell us your wife was a fallen woman, Mr Gorton!'' I can't put him through all that.'

'What does he think about it?' asked Petra.

'He doesn't know because I haven't told him.'

'About the transplant?'

'About any of it. About the baby or the transplant.'

Petra leant back in her chair wondering in what direction this conversation was leading.

'Are you saying, Mrs Gorton, that you're having second thoughts about the transplant? No one can force you to go ahead with it. But I must tell you that your son has just undergone another intensive course of chemotherapy to kill off his own diseased bone marrow in anticipation of receiving yours. It's a bit late in the day to pull out.'

Petra hoped she'd found the right combination of compassion, persuasion and firmness to force the point home. Heaven knew, she didn't want to antagonise the woman, but she was damned if she was going to let her walk out on the agreement without putting up a fight for David Smith.

'Of course I'm not saying that!' replied Andrea scornfully. 'What kind of person do you take me for? When I give my word I never go back on it. All I'm saying, Doctor, is that I don't want any personal contact with this young man. And I don't wish him to be referred to as my son at any point. No one in the hospital must know, for instance. Can you promise me that?'

'I'll certainly do my best to make sure that no one else knows,' replied Petra. 'I'll check on the hospital notes to see that there's nothing there that might refer to it. And I'll ask Dr Driscoll to pass on your wishes to David Smith so that he doesn't mention it inadvertently. It won't necessarily be assumed that you are related to him. Many people have bone marrow donated from complete strangers who just happen to be a close match.'

Andrea seemed satisfied by this assurance. 'That's fine, then,' she said. 'I'll just go home, pack my hospital bag and take a taxi to Milchester General.'

'What about your husband?' asked Petra. 'If you haven't told him about this, won't he be wondering why you're going into hospital?'

'Women's things…that's what I told him. And like most men of his generation he didn't wish to delve any further into it!' Andrea smiled at the recollection. 'He's at Westminster most of this week, and by the time he comes up at the weekend I should be back home and running round like a spring chicken.'

Two days later, Adam and Petra were visiting their 'bone-marrow' patients following the transplant which had taken place the previous day.

David Smith, after receiving his mother's bone marrow, was being nursed in an isolation ward and would be there for at least seventeen days. Andrea Gorton, depending on how well she was coping with the after-effects of the general anaesthetic and also how quickly she recovered from the bone-marrow extraction, could expect to be leaving hospital in a few days' time.

Adam went to speak to the senior house officer in charge of David's case, while Petra made her way to Andrea's room.

'How is Mrs Gorton?' she enquired of the ward sister.

'Doing very well, Doctor. She was a bit sore at the site of the extraction but we're giving her medication for that. And apart from looking pale, which is only to be expected in the short term, she's doing remarkably well. She's the wife of our local MP, you know.'

'Yes, I did know,' replied Petra cautiously.

'She's a very brave lady, isn't she? To donate bone marrow to a complete stranger, well, it's wonderfully public spirited and generous, isn't it?'

'Yes, it is.'

Petra followed the sister along the ward to a single-bedded room which she entered alone. Andrea was lying in bed, propped up on several pillows. Her normally ruddy complexion was now almost as white as the sheet she'd pulled up to her chin.

'How are you, Mrs Gorton?' Petra asked softly, sitting in a chair next to the bed. 'Sister tells me you're recovering well.'

'Fine,' she said in a hoarse voice. 'Just feel a bit wobbly. They walked me to the bathroom this morning and I felt a little weak. But the surgeon said I'll recover my strength in no time.'

'Good,' said Petra, patting the woman gently on the hand. 'Do you know when they'll let you home?'

'In a few days. When my husband gets back from London.'

'That's good. I'll be round to visit you and keep and eye on your blood count,' said Petra. 'You may need to take some extra iron pills and therapeutic vitamins if your cell count's a bit low. And try and avoid coming into contact with any coughs and sneezes for the next few weeks as you'll probably be more prone to infection for a short while, just until your bone marrow regenerates.'

Andrea nodded.

Petra rose to leave. 'Dr Driscoll and I are just going to call in and see our colleague, Dr Hughes, who's also a patient in the hospital. And Dr Driscoll is also here to see his patient, David Smith. He's in an isolation ward and so I expect he'll only be able to wave at him through a window!'

There was no response to this. Petra waited a moment before continuing. 'Did they tell you how the transplant went?'

'They said it went well. They said my bone marrow was very good quality. I said, "I bet you say that to all the donors!" But they insisted they didn't.'

'Dr Driscoll may have a message to pass on to you from David. Shall I come back with it if he has?'

'No, thank you, Doctor.' Andrea turned her face into the pillow and closed her eyes. Petra got the message that she was being dismissed.

She picked up her bag and walked out of Andrea's room. She checked with the nurse on duty as to which ward Adam's patient was in. Having been directed to one of the isolation wards, Petra set off, passing on the way a young woman with a fair-haired child.

'Is it all right if we come in?'

Andrea Gorton had barely closed her eyes after Petra's visit in an attempt to get some sleep. Was this yet another nurse coming in to check on her once again? How on earth could anyone get any rest in hospital when they were constantly waking you up?

'Come in,' she said drowsily, turning her head to

face her latest tormentor. To her surprise she saw it
wasn't a member of staff but a young woman with
a small child.

'I think you must be lost,' she said. 'There's only
me in here.'

'Are you Mrs Gorton?' the woman asked nervously. 'Mrs Andrea Gorton?'

'Yes, that's me.'

'Can we come in for a minute? You look very tired
so we won't stay long.'

The young woman came into the room, sat down
on the chair recently vacated by Dr Petra Phillips,
picked up the little girl and placed her on her knee.

The young woman was slim, with short dark hair.

The little girl was the kind of build Andrea would
have described as 'dainty'. She had straight blonde
hair and was dressed in a green velvet dress, white
socks and patent-leather shoes. Andrea noticed that
the child's eyes were green, just a shade lighter than
the velvet dress. She couldn't take her eyes off her.
She was so pretty, and so like...so like Rhodie. Tears
stung her eyes and she blinked them away.

'Oh, I'm so sorry,' said the young woman. 'We
didn't mean to upset you. Do you know who we are?
We won't stay long. I just wanted to say thank you.'

'Young lady, I have no idea who you are,' said
Andrea, feeling foolish for crying in front of this
complete stranger. It must be the after-effects of the
anaesthetic, she thought, making her feel weepy and
over-emotional. It was all because of the way this
little child was looking at her, so trustingly, with
those same big green eyes, just like her own little
sister used to do. The little sister who'd died.

Andrea realised with a shock that she hadn't

thought about Rhodie for a very long time. The memory of the loss was just too painful. She'd pushed it to the back of her mind like that other painful memory, the memory of being forced to give up her baby.

The young woman brushed a nervous hand through her short hair, making it temporarily stand on end.

'I'm Tess,' she said. 'David Smith's wife.'

If it had been possible for Andrea to go any paler she would have done.

'What do you want?' she asked through gritted teeth. 'Are you selling your story to the newspapers?'

The young woman looked puzzled. 'No,' she said, taken aback at the suggestion. 'I just wanted to come and see you and thank you with all my heart. Thank you for giving my husband the gift of life, which is what you've done. I know that you don't want him to contact you afterwards, and he'll respect your wishes. But I couldn't let the opportunity pass without letting you know what your generosity has meant to us. I know David isn't out of the woods yet. We've been told that the first hundred days are critical…and a certain percentage of transplants don't succeed. But without you he wouldn't even have got this far. He would have died. And now we have hope.'

For a few moments Andrea was so overcome with emotion she couldn't speak.

'Shall we go now, Pip?' Tess said to the small child.

'Stay,' said Andrea, fighting the urge to burst into tears again. 'Stay for a moment.'

She feasted her eyes on the two of them, but most of all at the little girl.

'It's Philippa's birthday today,' said Tess. 'She's three and she insisted on coming to see Daddy in her new party frock.'

'It's very pretty,' Andrea said to the small girl. 'It's a very pretty dress.'

She paused. 'I had a little sister who was the very image of you. And she had a green velvet dress which matched her eyes.'

'What was her name?' asked Philippa, overcoming her shyness.

'Rosemary. But she used to call herself Rhodie, so that's what we called her.'

'I call myself Pip because that's easier to say than Phiwip...' Struggling with the word at last, she announced triumphantly, 'Phiwippa.'

Tess hugged the child to her. 'That's really marvellous to know,' she said to Andrea. 'David and I often wondered where Pip got her unusual colouring from. We're both dark haired and blue-eyed. At least now we know that the blonde hair and green eyes came from his side of the family!'

'My grandmother, I believe, had the same colouring,' Andrea informed her. 'I've got an old photograph somewhere, but sadly they didn't have colour photography in those days and so it's just in black and white.'

'David will be so interested when I tell him!' Tess drew in her breath sharply. 'Oh, Mrs Gorton, you don't mind if I tell him, do you? I know what you said and everything...'

Andrea remained silent, thinking deeply about the implications. The silence was interrupted by Pip who had by now completely lost all trace of her earlier shyness.

'Where is this little girl?' she asked. 'The one who looks like me? Is she here?'

'No,' said Andrea kindly. 'She's in heaven.'

The child pondered for a moment. 'Like Grandma?'

'My mother passed away a few months ago,' explained Tess.

'I'm sorry,' said Andrea.

'I haven't got a grandma any more,' said Pip. 'But she's in heaven with that little girl who looks like me, isn't she?'

'Probably,' said Tess, realising the conversation could be turning slightly embarrassing. Both she and Andrea knew that the child *did*, in fact, have a grandmother, and that grandmother was Andrea.

'Guess what?' Tess said to Pip. 'The little girl who looked like you would have been Daddy's aunt. You know, like you have an Aunt Jane. Imagine that! Daddy didn't even know he had an aunt!'

The little girl jumped down from her mother's knee. 'Let's tell him now!' she enthused.

Tess leaned close to Andrea, whispering, 'Don't worry, we'll keep everything a secret. I know that you don't want any contact with David afterwards. We'll respect your wishes, Mrs Gorton. And I'm sorry if we upset you by coming.'

She followed the child towards the door.

Andrea watched them go.

'Come again,' she called after them weakly, hoping that her voice would carry. 'Come back again.'

*   *   *

Morning surgery was over and as it was getting near to lunchtime Petra decided to grab a sandwich at her desk and take the opportunity of catching up on her medical journals. There was a gentle knock on her door.

'Come in,' she said, her mouth full of tuna mayonnaise.

Adam popped his head round the door. 'Can I ask a favour?'

'Of course,' she said, beckoning him in.

'I'd like you to sign these passport photographs for me, please. You just have to write on the back that they're a true likeness, or words to that effect.' He placed two identical small colour photographs on top of one of her medical magazines.

She looked at them critically. They had obviously been taken in one of those instant photo booths and could hardly be described as flattering. She swallowed her mouthful of sandwich and wiped her hands on a tissue before picking them up and scrutinising them.

'I suppose that, at a pinch, they could just possibly be described as being a true likeness of you,' she said, 'but only just. Why don't you get some better ones done?'

'It's only for a passport, for heaven's sake. It's not meant to be a beauty contest.'

He produced a document and started looking through it. 'I think you have to write these particular words on the back,' he said to Petra. 'Sorry to barge in on your lunch-break, but I'd only just noticed that my passport is due to run out and I've got to get the thing signed by a professionally qualified person.'

'Doesn't that person have to have known you two years?' she asked.

'I'm not sure. I know it's different if it's a renewal of an existing passport. Just give me a second…' he said, quickly scanning through all the relevant small print.

Petra picked up her pen and waited for Adam to finish reading the form. She began to wonder why he had suddenly decidedly he needed a new passport in such a hurry. 'Planning a holiday abroad, are you?' she asked.

'No. But you never know, I might want to go abroad sooner rather than later. I don't want to get caught out.'

'You mean you're going to be working abroad again?'

'Who knows?' he replied enigmatically.

'Sounds to me as if you've decided already.' Petra's spirits took a dive. 'I thought you liked the practice.'

'I like the practice very much. I like Milchester very much.'

'So what's the problem? Is it anything I can help with?' Petra was surprised at how upset she was at the thought of Adam's departure.

'It's a personal matter,' he said, his voice noncommittal. 'Let's leave it at that.'

The phone rang.

'This might be Mark,' she said, picking it up. But instead of Mark's familiar voice it was a woman who spoke.

'Is that Petra Phillips?' she asked.

'Speaking.'

Adam indicated that he would leave, but Petra beckoned him back and, putting her hand over the mouthpiece, said, 'It's not Mark. Wait a moment and I'll do the pictures for you.'

Adam sat down again and continued reading the form.

'Sorry,' she said to the caller, 'what did you say your name was?'

'Melissa Footborough. I work with Mark.'

Petra took a sharp breath. 'There's nothing wrong, is there? He's not had an accident?'

'No, no,' she said. 'Nothing like that.'

Petra breathed a sigh a relief. She put her hand over the mouthpiece again and mouthed to Adam, 'Someone from Mark's office.'

'He's not had an accident,' said the girl at the other end of the phone. 'I'm ringing to speak to you because I'm worried about him.'

'Oh?'

'I don't know if you've noticed, but he's lost quite a bit of weight recently and he looks paler than he used to. I don't know if you've noticed that.'

'Yes, I have, actually. He told me it was because he's been working hard lately.'

'That's true enough,' said Melissa with a tinkling laugh. 'We're all working jolly hard. In particular on this Newmarket job.'

Petra's ears pricked up at the mention of Newmarket.

'Are you working with him on that job?' she asked, a picture beginning to form in her mind.

'As a matter of fact, I am,' said the caller. 'We've been spending an awful lot of time on it together, Mark and I. I don't know if he's mentioned me to you.'

'Your name doesn't ring a bell,' said Petra warily.

'We did go to Newmarket together because it's my father who's the racehorse trainer and that's why—'

'You went to Newmarket with Mark?' interrupted Petra.

'Yes. Didn't he say? I wonder why not?'

'I remember now,' said Petra, recovering her composure. 'He did mention you. And thank you for phoning with your concerns about my fiancé's health.'

'I thought, with you being a doctor and everything…'

'Precisely. I'm sure there's nothing to worry about, but thank you for getting in touch. I presume you don't want me to mention this phone call to Mark?'

The girl hesitated for a moment, then said, 'I don't mind if you do. You can tell him I rang if you like. Goodbye.'

Petra put the phone back on its cradle slowly and deliberately. 'I wonder what all that was about?'

'Want to talk about it or is it personal?' asked Adam.

'I'm not sure if it's personal or not,' she replied, puzzled by the phone call. 'What do you think? That was a woman called Melissa Footbridge or something like that. She works with Mark. In fact *she's* the woman he went to Newmarket with.'

'The one you mistakenly thought was having an affair with him?'

'The very one. She phoned to say she thought Mark was looking thinner and paler than usual. Which is true. I noticed it as well. But he assured me it was just the result of hard work and he was perfectly fit. In fact, only last week he went for his annual medical check-up and was declared absolutely fine. His blood pressure was up slightly but that was to be expected with him being under quite a lot of pressure at work at the moment.'

'So what was this Miss Footbridge's motive in phoning, do you think?'

'I have absolutely no idea.' Petra paused for a moment. 'Unless…unless she wants to make sure that I know of her existence.'

'You mean she's a troublemaker?'

'Could be.'

'Isn't she worried that you might mention the call to Mark?' asked Adam. 'Those kinds of people usually want to remain anonymous. They just want to stir things up a little.'

'Well, that's the strange thing,' said Petra. 'This Melissa seemed to be positively encouraging me to tell Mark about it. Almost as though that was the sole purpose of her phone call. Anyway,' she said briskly, 'what does it say in that passport application? Should I sign the photographs?'

'Not necessary,' he said, picking them up. 'If I'd read the form more thoroughly in the first place I needn't have bothered you. Apparently if you're just applying for a passport renewal, and your appearance hasn't changed much since the last time, you don't need anyone to sign it for you.'

As he walked to the door she couldn't stop herself saying, 'Don't leave us yet, will you?'

'You're a fine one to talk!' laughed Adam harshly. 'The moment you marry Mark you'll be off to London!'

'Oh, no!' she said, panic rising in her throat at the very thought. 'We're not moving to London straight away. It could be ages before we go. If at all.'

Adam's hand was on the doorhandle. 'Not having second thoughts, are you?'

'About moving to London? I've just told you it could be ages…'

He opened the door and stepped out into the corridor. 'I wasn't talking about that,' he said enigmatically, before shutting the door and walking away.

'So, what…?' Petra realised she was speaking to a closed door. So, what had he meant when he'd asked if she was having second thoughts? Had he meant, was she having second thoughts about marrying Mark? Was that what he'd meant?

She bit into her sandwich. Was she having second thoughts? Hell, of course she was. Getting married was a big step. Didn't everyone have second thoughts about it? It was only natural.

That evening at home she phoned Mark. She casually mentioned the intriguing call from one of his colleagues earlier in the day.

'Who was it?' he asked.

'Melissa Something-or-other. Sounded like Footbridge.'

'Footborough.'

'That's it. Melissa Footborough.'

There was a stunned silence at the other end of the phone.

'Mark, are you still there?'

He cleared his throat. 'Why did Melissa ring you?' he asked cagily.

'She thought you were looking thin.'

'Is that all?'

'Thin and pale.'

'I mean, is that all she phoned you about? My health?'

'I believe so,' said Petra. 'It's nice of her to be so concerned about you, isn't it?'

'She didn't say anything else?' Mark sounded defensive.

'Like what?'

'Oh, nothing. It seems a strange thing for her to do, that's all.'

'I thought so, too,' said Petra. Sensing his discomfort, she changed the subject. 'I spoke to your mother this morning. She told me she's going to be wearing peach.'

'Peach?' Mark sounded miles away.

'For the wedding. Her outfit is going to be peach.'

'Oh, the wedding,' said Mark. 'Of course.'

After her phone call to Mark, Petra looked idly out of her front window onto the street outside.

The nights were drawing in. The streetlamps were already lit and cars were driving past with their sidelights on. Out of the corner of one eye she saw a woman getting into a car that was parked further up the road and then drive off. As she passed in front of Petra's window she recognised her. It was the woman with the young child that Petra had seen visiting Adam some weeks ago. The child who called Adam 'Dadda'.

So, this was the woman in Adam's life! The woman who drove him abroad…the woman he came back for…and now, from what he'd said earlier, the woman who was behind his decision to work abroad again.

She must be a very special woman, said Petra to herself, fighting back the lump in her throat, if she can make him change his life so drastically at the drop of the hat. Or perhaps she's been using the child as a pawn, getting Adam to dance to her tune if he wanted to have access to his little boy. Manipulative, that's what some people were. And that probably goes for this Melissa Footborough—whoever she is and whatever she may or may not mean to Mark.

Petra pulled the curtains closed and switched on the TV. There were game shows on at least two channels and soaps on two of the others.

'Good,' she said, settling into a comfortable chair. 'Just what I need to take me out of myself… something totally uncomplicated and mindless.'

CHAPTER NINE

LATE summer was turning into autumn and the countdown to the wedding—only four months away—had taken over the hearts and minds of her nearest and dearest. Petra's mother was deeply immersed in wedding plans almost to the exclusion of everything else. And her father was no better.

'It's very important to pick the right photographer,' he said one evening when Petra was staying the weekend with them. 'You don't want some blundering idiot who misses out on the best shots. On the other hand, you don't want a bossy-boots who throws his weight around and virtually takes over the whole proceedings!'

Petra and her mother exchanged knowing looks. They each knew that her father was blatantly overreacting to his role as father of the bride—and they loved him for it.

'Dad, I'm sure you'll come up with exactly the right choice,' said Petra, barely disguising her amusement.

'It's all right for you to smile, young lady,' said her father, waving a sheaf of photographers' brochures at her. 'It's a very important day for an old buffer like me. It's not every day that I get to walk my only child down the aisle and give her away. Finding the right man to capture the momentous event on film and video is almost as important as you finding the right man to marry!'

The words were barely out of his mouth before he realised how absurd they sounded, and all three of them burst into peals of laughter.

'Which reminds me, Petra,' said her mother, wiping away her tears of mirth, 'what time are you meeting Mark tonight?'

Petra checked the time on the mantelpiece clock. 'Any minute now.' As she spoke the doorbell rang.

Mark was also staying in the village with his parents this weekend, with the express purpose of finalising the names on their wedding invitation list.

He came in for a moment to say 'hello' to his future in-laws before he and Petra walked to the Church Inn. They sat in a cosy corner of the village pub which faced the beautiful sixteenth century church where their marriage was going to take place in the New Year.

Petra was glad to note that Mark hadn't lost any more weight recently, but he still had that haunted expression she'd noticed for some weeks.

'Still busy at work?' she enquired when they were settled at the table with their drinks.

'Getting better,' he replied. 'I've asked to be given more client work based in Milchester.'

'Oh, that's good,' said Petra, hoping that this meant a change of heart for Mark and that he wouldn't be so keen on a permanent move to London after they were married.

'I suppose so,' said Mark, his voice flat and expressionless.

Petra took a good look at him. True, he didn't look ill but there was something the matter, she was sure of it. Possibly not anything to do with his health, but whatever it was it had produced a profound change in her fiancé—not only in his appearance but in his personality, too. He was a shadow of his former confident self.

'OK,' she said, putting down the notepad on which they were going to start writing out their wedding guest list. 'Spill the beans, Mark. Tell me exactly what's going on.'

'What do you mean?' he asked, barely able to meet her gaze. 'There's nothing going on. I promise you. There never has been.'

A mist was slowly beginning to lift from her eyes and she felt she was on the verge of a momentous discovery. Momentous for their future together. 'Are you referring to other relationships?' she asked.

He turned red-rimmed eyes on her. 'Look, Petra, I can handle it. It won't affect anything. I'm a man of honour, a man of my word. You can trust me, you know that.'

Petra stared out of the pub window and across the village green to the floodlit church.

She knew. She just knew.

'You've fallen in love with someone else.' It was a statement, not a question. 'It's that Melissa Footbridge woman, isn't it?'

'Footborough,' he corrected. The abject misery in his voice exactly matched the look on his face.

'Oh, Mark,' whispered Petra, reaching out a hand to him. 'What's going on?'

'You're right,' he said after a lengthy pause. 'Melissa and I did fall in love. But we realised it was only a passing phase. Well, at least I did. Melissa has taken it hard, the fact that I'm still going to marry you.'

'You're planning to marry me when you're in love with another woman?' Petra was incredulous.

'It was a passing phase, I tell you. An impulsive action. We were spending so much time working together on a particular project…and it just happened. Or, rather, nothing happened. I made sure of that. We didn't sleep together if that's what you're thinking.'

'And this was when you went to Newmarket?' she asked quietly, the pieces of the jigsaw beginning to form a picture.

Mark nodded. 'We fought our feelings. I told her that I'm marrying you. That you are the love of my life. End of story.' He picked up his beer and buried his face in the glass as if once again he wished to avoid her eyes.

It was the first time Mark had said those words…that she was the love of his life…and they had a distinctly hollow ring, as if he was trying to convince himself as much as anyone.

Petra reached out to him again, feeling no anger for the man, only deep pity.

'You love her, don't you? You're still in love with her.'

He sighed deeply.

'Perhaps,' he admitted at last. 'But I've told her it's over. It all came to a head after she'd phoned you on the pretext of asking you about my health. I realised then that she was trying to cause trouble between us. Between you and me.'

'It was only natural,' said Petra. 'I'd have done the same myself.'

'Would you?'

'If the man I loved was getting away from me, I'd

most certainly put up a fight for him. That's all
Melissa was doing. And at least it brought it out into
the open.'

'So what should we do?' Mark was uncharacter-
istically wavering, unsure of the next move.

'We'll call off the wedding,' said Petra. 'You go
back to London and take up your relationship with
Melissa. It'll all be for the best. Believe me, Mark,
I know about these things.'

The irony of using one of Mark's pet phrases
wasn't lost on him and he managed a weak smile.
He looked like a man who had just had an enormous
weight lifted from his shoulders.

'What about you, Petra? I feel I've let you down
badly. All those years we've been friends…we can't
just throw them away.'

'We don't have to. We'll still be friends.' She bit
her lip to hold back the emotion she could feel well-
ing up inside her. She stood up. 'I'd like to go home
now,' she said, her voice quavering.

Petra drove back to Milchester that evening, leaving
her parents stunned by the news. She felt unable to
face spending the rest of the weekend looking at their
distraught faces. They'd get over it, she said to herself as she drove back into the city.

It wasn't until she was safely inside her own little
town house that she allowed herself the luxury of
wallowing in her misery. The strange thing was, she
discovered that she wasn't half as miserable as she'd
imagined she'd be. Relief was what she mainly felt.
Relief that she and Mark had realised before it had
been too late that, although they were good friends,
they were unlikely to have had a good marriage.

She was also glad that Mark hadn't picked up her remark, 'If the man I loved was getting away from me I'd put up a fight for him.' Well, he was getting away from her—and yet she wasn't inclined to put up a fight for him. Now, why was that?

She picked up the phone and dialled a number she knew off by heart.

'Adam,' she said when he answered, 'I know it's late but can I come round for a little while? I don't want to be alone right now.'

'Sure,' he said without hesitation. 'I'll be standing outside, waiting for you.'

'I wonder if I was ever really in love with Mark,' said Petra, in confessional mood after two coffees and a couple of restorative brandies.

'When you've known someone for a long time,' said Adam, 'it's hard to distinguish between true love and comfortable friendship.'

'You're right. It's very hard and I'm very confused. I *did* love him, but I don't know if I was *in love* with him,' she said, beginning to experience a delayed reaction and allowing a small teardrop to run down her cheek.

Adam moved over to the sofa where she was sitting and slid a comforting arm round her.

'When you're in love you become obsessed with the other person and you can't bear to be without them. Is that how it was for you and Mark? Did you fall asleep thinking of him?' he asked softly. 'Did you wake up thinking about him?'

She put her head in her hands in a gesture of confusion. 'Oh Adam, you seem to know so much about it. It's obvious that you've been in love.' She felt his arm tighten around her.

'Yes, I have,' he said softly. 'I still am.'

So she'd been right, thought Petra! There was a woman, or a wife, in Adam's life for whom he still held a candle. He was confirming her worst fears and it was as if someone had thrown a bucket of cold water over her. Ever since she'd met him, she now admitted, she'd been obsessed with him. It was he, not Mark, who was the one she thought about last thing at night and first thing in the morning. It was Adam whom she dreamed about. According to his reckoning, that meant she was in love with him.

Of course she was! She'd known it all along. And like Mark with Melissa, she had tried to convince herself that it wasn't true, that it was a passing phase, because she'd been engaged to another man. But now that she and Mark were no longer engaged she could view her feelings for Adam in a completely different light.

Admit it, she told herself, you're deeply attracted to the man. You shamelessly fantasise about him, imagining what it would be like if he made love to you. You constantly relive each of his kisses in sensual slow motion and make every excuse to be in his presence. And yet at the very moment you admit you're in love with the man, he confirms he's in love with someone else!

Life's a bitch.

In the early hours of the morning Adam walked Petra the short distance to her door. He kissed her gently and chastely on the cheek before returning to his own town house.

He felt very proud of himself for his actions or, more accurately, for his inactions. There was nothing he wanted more, on hearing that Mark was no longer on the scene, than to sweep her in his arms and ask her to stay the night with him. He believed she wouldn't have needed much persuading. But he wasn't minded to take advantage of her when she was at a low ebb and vulnerable. Much better to play it softly, softly, allowing her the space and time to get over her broken engagement.

As he climbed into bed his eye caught sight of the notepad on his bedside table. On it was Harry's phone number. Harry, the friend and senior medic he'd kept in touch with from his days in Bosnia.

'If ever you're thinking of working overseas again, give me a call,' he'd said when Adam had returned to England.

Adam had made that call a few days ago.

Harry had been delighted to hear from him. 'Just the chap we need. How soon can you get here?'

Adam had been hesitant to make the decision there and then. He'd told his former medical colleague that he needed to think about it for a short while before giving notice to quit his Milchester post. Petra's news had put everything in a different light. Thank goodness he hadn't done anything irrevocable! The main reason—in fact, the only reason—he was planning on leaving was because he had no wish to be around to see the woman he loved marry someone else. Today's turn of events put a whole new complexion on things.

As his head hit the pillow a smile danced on his lips. How he wished she was with him right now! His mind throbbed with images of the two of them in bed together, moving in slow, sensual delight, their hearts beating in unison, their bodies pulsing to the same fevered pace. God, he was desperate for her!

But don't rush her, he told himself. He had to give her enough time to get over Mark. He'd give her lots of time…until tomorrow, anyway. He'd waited long enough and couldn't bear to wait any longer. Tomorrow, he determined, tomorrow he'd go into action.

The next morning, Petra was kept so busy she had no time to dwell on her emotional problems.

It was her turn to do the radio phone-in and thankfully no one at the radio station remarked on her missing engagement ring. She felt she'd have a much better chance of getting over the whole episode if it wasn't mentioned by anyone. A forlorn hope, she knew. Once back at the medical centre it was bound to be noticed by the receptionist and the other partners. Unless Adam had got in first and told them not to say anything. But why should he? It was unlikely that Adam should want to protect her feelings when he had another relationship on his mind.

Just as she was leaving the radio station her mobile rang. It was Rhoda Redfern, the actress from *Jackson's Market*.

'Can you come round to the TV studios now, Doctor?' asked Rhoda. 'There's been a small accident and one of the actors has cut his leg. I told the producer how good you are at stitching up wounds and all that sort of thing, and he asked if I'd give you a ring.'

'If it's a bad cut, shouldn't you be taking him to the hospital?' enquired Petra, not unreasonably.

'That's just it,' replied Rhoda. 'It isn't terribly bad

but may just need a stitch or two. As for taking Bill to the hospital, well, you can wait there for hours, can't you? And that would disrupt the filming schedule.'

'Don't you have a medical officer on call?' asked Petra, surprised that a large TV company didn't have that particular facility.

'We have a nurse in what is laughingly called our medical centre,' replied Rhoda scornfully. 'But even if she could cope with this, which I doubt, she's on her day off! Please, come, Doctor. I'm sure we can come to some arrangement about fees and that sort of thing.'

'That wasn't my primary concern,' replied Petra, hoping that her hesitation about getting involved didn't appear to be for mercenary reasons. 'I'm on my way.'

Petra phoned the surgery to tell them where she was going before driving the short distance across town to the TV studios.

'Well done,' said the receptionist who answered her call. 'Dr Michaels has been trying to get in with the TV company for ages. He'd like a nice little contract with them, to be on call and that kind of thing. Wouldn't do our budget any harm if you could fix it,' she hinted gleefully.

'This is just a one-off emergency call,' said Petra, hating the idea of touting for business.

On arriving at the studios she was taken straight to the outdoor set and introduced to the producer.

'Rhoda tells me you're a miracle-worker,' he said, dazzling her with his smile. 'But, then, she is an actress and much given to exaggeration. I'd be grateful for something less than a miracle.'

'What's the problem?' she asked, following him across the cobbled street.

'The actor who plays Porky Paterson had a small accident this morning,' replied the producer. 'He refused to let us call an ambulance. He's now sitting bleeding in the green-room like the trouper that he is.'

He led her to a room off the main set where an older man was sitting, clutching a blood-soaked pad to his calf.

'This is Dr Phillips, Bill,' said the producer. 'She's come to take a look at your leg.'

'That's what all you young ladies say,' chirped Bill, giving Petra a cheeky wink. 'Can't wait to get the clothes off me!'

Petra laughed. She recognised the actor who played the part of an extremely scruffy individual. She was surprised at his voice which was quite unlike that of the character, Porky Paterson, which he played using a very thick Lancashire accent.

'How did you cut yourself?' she asked.

'On a jagged bit of metal no one noticed until I backed into it,' he said, annoyance creeping into his voice. 'I've got a feeling that someone from the scenery department is going to have his hands smacked very hard.'

'Right.' Petra bent down for a closer examination. She removed the blood-soaked pad, which had been covering an area of torn material, and saw a jagged cut. A small trickle of blood oozed out.

'I'll need to cut this off,' she said to Bill, indicating the torn trouser leg. 'And I'll have to clean the wound and stitch it. Is there somewhere with a wash basin and, ideally, more sterile conditions that this place?'

The green-room contained a few dilapidated chairs and a Formica table with a collection of used coffee-mugs and a large, catering-sized flask.

'The make-up department is very near,' said the producer. 'That's much more hygienic than this.'

He and Petra helped Bill out of his chair and then, with their arms around him, guided him to the make-up department and sat him down in a chair next to a wash-basin. The make-up artist brought some clean towels. After cutting away the bottom half of his trouser leg, she began to clean and dress the wound.

A production assistant who had followed them in watched the costume being cut and said, 'I'll get on to Wardrobe and see if I can find Bill another pair of trousers. I just hope it doesn't affect continuity. The director's a stickler for good continuity.'

As she left, the producer turned to Petra. 'Hope you don't think we're a callous bunch, worrying about continuity when a man's leg could be at stake.'

'I don't think the leg is at stake this time,' said Petra. 'I just hope you're covered for tetanus, Bill.'

'You bet,' said the actor. 'With the filthy costumes I have to wear as Porky Paterson, I take no chances.'

On hearing this, the make-up girl was shocked. 'It's not real dirt in the costumes, Bill. You know that! It's only paint and powder made to look dirty.'

'I'm taking no chances.'

'Very wise,' said Petra, 'as it has proved today. That was a nasty cut, and quite deep.' She finished stitching and put her suture pack back in her bag. 'I'd better call in tomorrow and take a look at it.'

'Thanks, Doc,' said Bill gratefully.

'Yes, many thanks,' reiterated the producer. 'Now, about payment...this is obviously classed as private work for you. I spoke to our financial director before you arrived and he agrees that we need to have a medic on call for the times when our nurse is unable to deal with a particular situation. He wants to put the arrangement on a proper footing. Can he speak to you about it?'

Petra picked up her bag, ready to leave. 'Dr Michaels, my senior partner, is the man he should speak to. He deals with all financial matters.' She scribbled down the phone number and handed it to him.

'That's great,' said the producer. 'And many thanks for coming here at such short notice.'

'See you tomorrow, Bill,' she said.

She was escorted off the film set and again met the production assistant who waved a pair of extremely dirty-looking trousers at her. 'Brilliant match,' she said. 'It'll take a very keen-eyed viewer to spot the switch.'

When Petra finally arrived back at the medical centre, Adam popped his head round her door.

'Dinner tonight?' he asked.

'Er, I'm not sure,' replied Petra.

'Are you otherwise engaged? Oops, didn't mean to say that.'

'I'm not sensitive about it,' she lied. 'You don't have to avoid using the word "engaged" in my presence!'

'In that case, are you coming out with me tonight? There's this wonderful new Nepalese restaurant in town called the Third Eye. Do you fancy it?'

When she didn't reply straight away, Adam stepped inside and closed the door behind him.

'Is it too soon?' he asked. 'Too soon after your broken engagement? Is that why you're hesitant?'

'That's not the reason,' she answered truthfully.

'In that case, say you'll come. Please.' He looked so appealing, almost boyish. 'No strings attached. Just two friends going out for a meal. Nothing wrong in that, is there?'

'No. I mean, yes, I'll come.'

He'd worn her down. To refuse to go out for a meal with him would have been churlish and achieved nothing. If he had another woman in his life then at least Petra was well aware of it. And he knew she knew because he'd told her so himself. So why not go out for a friendly meal, as long as she made it clear that this was all it was going to be? And, of course, Adam had in recent times behaved impeccably. Even last night, when he might have succeeded in getting her into bed with him, he hadn't so much as kissed her on the mouth. That was certainly not the way he'd behaved on the previous occasion when he'd believed her engagement was off. Many times, particularly as she'd been drifting off to sleep, she'd recalled that encounter in the car park when he'd kissed her with such passion and she'd responded like a wild animal, wanting him more than she'd ever wanted any man.

'Pick you up at eight,' he said, leaving her room quickly, as if he believed Petra might change her mind if he stayed a moment longer.

When Adam called for her that evening she thought he looked even more handsome than ever—a thrill-

ing combination of experienced manliness and boyish vulnerability.

She noticed with pleasure the way his eyes swept
over her body in an appreciative manner. She was
glad she'd dressed up, choosing to wear an elegant
amber dress instead of the black trousers and white
silk shirt she'd originally decided on. She was aware
that the dress suited her, clinging in all the right
places, the colour picking up the subtle amber high-
lights of her naturally blonde hair.

The restaurant and the food turned out to be every
bit as good as he'd promised. His relaxed, amiable
manner made the evening more enjoyable than she
would have believed possible under the circumstances. All her troubles seemed to melt to nothing
in the warmth of his engaging smile.

Throughout the evening he kept away from any
subject he knew would cause her anxiety, never once
mentioning her former fiancé or the aborted wedding.
They discovered a mutual love of poetry, an interest
that she and Mark had never shared. He had even
tried his hand at writing poetry, Adam told her. 'But
I gave up when I realised that others had done it so
much better.'

'That was a delicious meal,' she said later as they
walked back from the car park and were approaching
Adam's front door. 'I obviously haven't let the broken engagement affect my appetite.'

'Come in for a nightcap,' he said, slipping an arm
around her and guiding her towards his town house.

She seemed hesitant.

'Just a teeny-weeny one,' he said, indicating the
smallness of the drink between his thumb and index
finger.

'That wasn't why I was hesitating,' she said.

'Then what's the reason? What are you worrying about?' The look on his face was genuine.

She couldn't bring herself to say, 'I'm not coming in for a nightcap because I think I might end up in bed with you!' That would have been just too presumptuous—and, in any event, Adam might not be intending even to flirt with her, let alone make love to her. After all, recently he'd barely touched her in a sexual way.

And so, not wishing to appear foolish, she said, 'I'm not worrying about anything. I'd love a nightcap so long as it's a black coffee.'

'It'll keep you awake, you know.' He put the key in the latch.

'That's the idea.' She laughed.

In Adam's living room there was a thick-pile rug in front of an open fire. It wasn't a real open fire but one of those gas fires with lifelike pieces of coal. All the new town houses on their block had them and when the lights in the room were dimmed they looked very attractive, almost like the real thing.

She sat down on the sofa and while Adam went into the kitchen to make the coffee, she surreptitiously surveyed the room and the various pictures and photographs which were placed on tables and hung on walls.

She'd been in Adam's house yesterday but hadn't noticed any of them. She'd been far too caught up in her broken engagement—and after several brandies she hadn't been able to remember much about anything, let alone Adam's furnishings and decor.

The pictures, she noted, were unremarkable reproduction prints and had probably come with the house when Adam had rented it. The framed photographs, three in total, were of far more interest to her. She leaned forward in order to get a better look at them.

One was an old sepia-toned photograph of a man, who looked very like Adam and was dressed in army uniform. Possibly his father, or even grandfather, she surmised. Next to it was a colour picture of an elderly couple standing in the garden of a delightful old thatched cottage. Again, possibly his parents or grandparents.

The next picture, of a woman and child, made her almost slide off the edge of the sofa as she strained forward to scrutinise it.

It was her! The woman she'd seen visiting Adam on at least two occasions. And on her knee was the little boy who called Adam 'Dadda'.

She heard Adam's footsteps and guiltily sat back on the sofa, pretending to be reading a medical magazine she'd found on a side table.

'Stop that straight away,' he ordered playfully, handing her a mug of coffee. 'This is your time off, so no boning up on heart bypass procedures.'

Petra looked up at him, his face relaxed and handsome in the soft light. The dark blue of his shirt toned in beautifully with his tan. He sat down on the rug, kicking off his loafers and loosening his silk tie. Previously he'd removed his jacket and flung it unceremoniously over a chair.

'Don't know why I put on all this formal gear—suit, tie, shirt. I expect it's because I can't ever forget that I could be called out professionally at any moment and patients expect doctors to wear suits, not T-shirts.'

'You're not on call tonight, are you?'

'No.'

'Me neither. I just wondered why you thought you might be called out.'

'Force of habit, I suppose.' Adam took a sip of his coffee. 'Sure you won't have a brandy?'

She shook her head. 'I remember what happened last night…three big ones! I've still got the headache to prove it.'

Adam smiled. Then he gazed at her more seriously. 'How are you feeling? I'm not talking about the brandy, I mean the broken engagement.'

'Getting over it,' she replied. 'In fact, I'm beginning to feel guilty about just how quickly I'm getting over it. Which only goes to prove that Mark wasn't the right man for me anyway.'

'Don't feel guilty,' said Adam. 'All's fair in love and war. I should know, I've been in both of them!'

'Tell me,' said Petra, 'tell me about why you went to Bosnia. You once said it was because of a woman.'

She knew she was treading on dangerous ground but she had to know the truth. Adam had avoided telling her about the woman in his life, the one he was still in love with, and she was going to have it out with him even at the risk of being told to mind her own business.

Adam paused before he answered, gathering his thoughts. 'I was in a very similar situation to you,' he said. 'Jenny and I had known each other for years. Grown up together, like you and Mark. We became engaged one Christmas because we thought it was a very romantic thing to do. I was devastated when she broke it off. Well, more hurt pride than devastated.

But I know she did the right thing. We just wouldn't have been right for each other.'

Petra carefully put down her empty coffee mug. 'Is that when you decided to join the Foreign Legion?'

Adam laughed. 'That was my knee jerk reaction. When I'd calmed down I realised that she'd done me a favour, a great favour. So I didn't join the Foreign Legion. I went instead to Bosnia.'

'You said you were still in love with her.' Petra shot him an accusing look.

Adam shook his head. 'I wasn't talking about Jenny.'

'And what about your son?' In for a penny, in for a pound, decided Petra. Let's get to the bottom of Adam's private life…he knows everything about mine. She pointed to the photograph on the table behind him.

He swung round and picked up the picture to which she'd been referring.

'You mean Daniel.' Adam gazed indulgently at the image of the child. 'Little Danny's the reason I came back from Bosnia.'

'So you have a son?' Petra attempted to keep her voice light and unaccusing. It was none of her business if he chose not to mention the fact that he had a child. A little odd, though.

'Danny's not my son,' he replied. 'Why would you think he was? I would certainly have told you about something that important.'

'But I saw you with him,' stumbled Petra, beginning to wonder if he was a liar. 'I was watching from an open window and I heard him call you Daddy!'

Adam threw his head back and guffawed. 'Dadda,

that's what he calls me! It's the best stab at saying Adam that my small nephew can make.'

'*Nephew*,' repeated Petra, feeling foolish. 'And this woman is…'

'My sister. Who did you think she was?'

'Your wife,' replied Petra. After a pause she went on, 'Well, you must admit you kept your private life very private, very secretive. "I came back from Bosnia for personal reasons"…all that kind of thing. No wonder some of us jumped to the wrong conclusions!'

He put the picture back on the table and moved to the sofa, seating himself next to Petra.

'Sorry,' he said. 'I didn't mean to be secretive. It was just the way things were at the time I came back.'

'There you go again, talking in riddles. I've still no idea why you came back! Why *did* you?'

A flicker of pain briefly crossed his face. 'It was Danny. My sister wrote and told me that he'd been diagnosed with leukaemia and she had been tested as a prospective bone-marrow donor but had sadly turned out not to be a good match. She asked if I would be tested on the off chance that my tissue type would provide a good match.'

'And it was?'

'Amazingly good, considering that I'm only his uncle and not a sibling. I came home straight away and the transplant was performed. I decided to stay in England for several months to be on hand in case there was any need for a further transplant, and to give my sister moral and physical support. She's a single parent—her husband walked out on her when she was pregnant. Hated kids, he said.'

Petra was shocked. 'Who would behave like that?'

'A complete bastard, that's who,' said Adam with some bitterness.

'Your poor sister,' she said with feeling. 'And then, after all that, to discover that her child had leukaemia! Is he all right now, your little nephew?'

'Fingers crossed,' said Adam. 'The first months were critical, but the most critical time was after about three weeks. It was then that the transplanted bone marrow should start to take and begin producing blood cells. We cracked open the champagne on that day, I can tell you!'

'Ah,' said Petra, 'that's why you knew so much about bone-marrow transplants when David Smith's case came up.'

He nodded. 'First-hand knowledge, you might say.'

'So why didn't you tell us you'd been through it all yourself? Was it all too emotional for you?'

Adam considered this for a moment. 'In a way,' he said. 'My main reason for being reluctant to talk about it was…well, it sounds as if I'm making myself out to be a big hero when all I did was what anyone would have done in similar circumstances. Even Andrea Gorton!'

Petra leaned towards him, an enticing smile playing on her lips. 'Well, I think you're a hero.'

He touched her face with his strong fingers, moving himself closer to her. 'If I'm a hero to you, Petra, what more could I want?' His voice was husky and full of desire.

He kissed her on the lips and she felt a familiar thrill race through her. She put a hand to his cheek and stroked the hard angles of it, loving the faint prickling of his stubbled chin against her own.

'I forgot to shave,' he whispered in her ear.

'It's nice,' she said, her heart racing as a sensual beat started deep inside her body.

He placed his arms around her and felt her shudder. His own body stirred with arousal, heat burning under his skin. He kissed her neck and moved his lips downwards towards the twin mounds of her breasts. His fingers expertly unhooked the fastener at the back of her dress and slowly, seductively, began to undress her.

His mouth nuzzled her neck and a hand cupped one of her naked breasts. Her own hands flew to his chest as she undid his shirt buttons with a speed she'd not known she was capable of.

Then the phone rang.

'Damn,' he swore. 'Shall we ignore it?' But even as he said it he knew he never could. He was a doctor and this could be an emergency even though he wasn't on call tonight.

It was the ring of a mobile phone and he began to search for it in his jacket pocket. But when he pulled it out it wasn't his phone that was doing the ringing.

'Blast,' Petra. 'Must be mine.'

She searched around for her handbag, following the insistent sound of the ringing in order to locate the bag, which was lying partly hidden under the sofa.

'Dr Phillips,' she said, answering the call. She shivered, beginning to feel the chill in her present state of undress. Adam slipped his jacket over her naked shoulders.

'Oh, hello, Dad,' she said, sitting back on the sofa as she took in her father's news.

Adam picked up the coffee-mugs and left the room to give Petra privacy for her phone call. When he returned a few minutes later he found Petra standing up, dressed and looking very pale. She was putting the mobile phone back into her handbag.

'Anything the matter?' he asked.

'It's my mother,' answered Petra, her voice choking with anxiety. 'She's had a stroke.'

'Oh, no,' he said, rushing to her side and putting a comforting arm round her. 'How is she?'

'They're not sure. They've brought her in to Milchester General. Dad's with her. He said she had a funny turn earlier this evening, collapsed on the kitchen floor. She felt dizzy and said there was a numbness down one side of her body. She also had a temporary loss of vision and her speech was slurred. Oh, hell, Adam, it's all my fault!'

'How can you say that? You've been with me all evening. And your father did the right thing by getting her to hospital. I don't see how you could have done anything, not being there…'

'I mean it's my fault because I caused it!' Petra said miserably. 'It must have been the shock of the broken engagement, calling the wedding off and all that sort of thing. I'd been so wrapped up in my own problems that I hadn't give much thought to how it must have affected my parents. They were so looking forward to the wedding, then having to cancel all the arrangements they'd made… It's no wonder my mother had a stroke. It's a wonder my father hasn't had a cardiac arrest for the same reason—he was getting very deeply into wedding mode. And now, on top of the cancellation, he's got my mother to worry about.' She sighed deeply. 'I tell you, it's all my fault.'

She was shaking with the shock of the bad news. Adam was still holding her tightly. If he let go he was convinced she'd fall over because she was shaking so much.

'It's not your fault,' he said gently. 'It can happen at any time, to anyone—you know that. And with your father being a doctor, she couldn't have had a better person on hand at the time.'

She looked up at him, grateful for the reassurance. 'I suppose so,' she agreed. 'I'm going to the hospital now. I'll call a taxi because I don't fancy walking to the car park on my own at this time of night.'

'I'll drive you there,' said Adam. 'I wouldn't dream of letting you go there alone.'

He picked up his jacket and walked with her to the front door. As they passed the hall table, her eyes took in the detail on a buff envelope. It was official-looking with 'On Her Majesty's Service' stamped at the top.

'Your call-up papers?' she joked, nervous anxiety about her mother making her seem light-headed and almost flippant.

'It's my passport stuff,' he said as they left the house. 'I'll deal with it later.'

Oh, yes, I remember. Adam's getting a job abroad, she said to herself, a numbness creeping over her as she prepared to hear some bad news about her mother.

At the hospital the receptionist told them which ward had admitted Petra's mother. Hurrying along, Petra found herself nearly breaking into a run, she was walking so quickly.

She spotted her father, waving to her down one end of a corridor.

'Oh, Dad,' she said, running into his open arms. Adam joined them a few moments later.

'This is my partner from the practice, Dr Adam Driscoll,' she said, introducing him to her father.

'How is Mrs Phillips?' Adam asked.

'Dad just told me that they don't really know yet.' Tears began to trickle down her cheeks.

'My wife is going to need some tests,' said Petra's father. 'Just the usual things in a case like this—blood tests and a scan to find out if the stroke is due to an intra-cerebral haemorrhage or a thrombosis. Or anything else.'

Petra and Adam knew exactly what he meant by 'anything else'. His unspoken concern was that his wife might be suffering from a brain tumour, but no one mentioned the dreaded words.

'Is she conscious?' asked Adam.

'Semi-conscious, at the moment,' he replied. 'She drifted in and out of consciousness while we were waiting for the ambulance.'

'When did it happen?' asked Petra.

'About two hours ago. She was in the kitchen, making the cocoa before we went to bed. Thank goodness I hadn't gone up first or I might not have seen her collapse.'

Petra turned to Adam. 'I'd like to stay here and just wait and see how things progress…be with her…' She didn't add 'in case she dies', but the words hung unspoken in the air.

'Sure,' said Adam, giving her hand a squeeze. 'I'll

leave now but give me a call if you need me. And don't worry about the practice. We'll cover for you or get someone in if necessary.'

Petra and her father sat on either side of her mother's bed. They were each holding one of her hands.

The news had been good. The diagnosis was that Mrs Phillips had suffered a transient ischaemic attack, a kind of mini-stroke. It was predicted that she would make a full recovery. The specialist in charge of Mrs Phillips's case had told them that the danger of any further attacks could be greatly reduced by taking an anticoagulant drug or aspirin.

'Home soon,' said her mother in a weak voice. She hadn't fully recovered her powers of speech but she'd been assured that this would come right in time.

'We're arranging nursing help for a short time so that you can come home sooner—and I'll take a few days off work as well. Once we've got you in your own surroundings you'll come along in leaps and bounds,' Petra assured her.

'Silly fool,' said her mother crossly.

'Who? Me?' asked Petra, surprised at the venom in her mother's voice.

'No. Me. Silly old fool. Having this stupid stroke.' She struggled with the words, determined to get them out.

Petra looked across the bed to her father. 'I do feel terribly guilty, Dad. I'm sure it was my fault, the broken engagement and everything. It must have come like a bolt from the blue. Do you think it was the shock?'

'No, dear,' he said kindly. 'I'm sure it was nothing

to do with that. Transient ischaemic attacks just happen. We doctors know that, don't we? If anyone should be feeling guilty it's me. I was so involved with wedding arrangements I hadn't given a moment's thought to the inner torment you must have been going through. There was I, worrying about choosing the right man to take the photographs, and all the time you must have been going through hell, wondering if you'd chosen the right man to marry! I even made some awful joke about it. I now see that was in very bad taste.'

Petra realised that her father was being kind, absolving her of any blame for her mother's stroke, and she was grateful to him for it.

CHAPTER TEN

THE news about Petra's mother continued to be good. She was making excellent progress and there was no recurrence of the transient ischaemic attack.

Petra, who had sat by her mother's bedside throughout the night and into the next day, decided she'd slip home for a short time to have a shower, a change of clothes and a quick meal. Her father couldn't be persuaded to do the same.

'Not yet. I've lost my appetite for the moment, love. I'll grab a sandwich from the hospital canteen if I change my mind.'

She returned to the hospital a couple of hours later, having first phoned the practice and spoken to Don.

'Adam told us what happened last night,' he said, offering his good wishes for her mother's speedy recovery.

'Thanks, Don,' she said. 'I'm going to need to take some time off when she comes home. I'd like to be there to look after her for a few days and to be a support for her and my father.'

'No problem,' assured Don. 'Hannah rang this morning to say she's desperate to get back to work, even if it's only part time. I was thinking of cutting down on Helen's hours, but I won't do that until you come back.'

'That's good news about Hannah,' said Petra, relieved that her partner had got over her injuries so quickly. 'The last time I spoke to her was when she'd been home a short time and she sounded very bored. Said she couldn't wait to get back. And I'm so pleased about Helen, too. She's a terrific locum.'

'Indeed,' replied Don. 'Pity we haven't got anything more permanent we can offer her.'

Petra had to bite her tongue to stop herself blurting out, 'We'll have a vacancy soon. Adam's leaving to work abroad.'

'And by the way,' added Don as an afterthought, 'well done with your Porky Paterson connection. As a result we're now negotiating a nice little contract with the TV company.'

Mention of the TV company reminded Petra. 'I was meant to be checking on the actor today, but someone else will have to do it.'

'No problem there,' assured Don. 'Adam did your calls this morning. Apparently Porky Paterson, or whatever his name is, was very disappointed that it wasn't you calling to see him. He's obviously taken quite a shine to you!'

Petra laughed. 'You can't believe a word these actors say. They're so used to playing a part that you never know which is their true face.'

She replaced the receiver. Wasn't that true of someone else? Someone she thought she knew well...Adam Driscoll. He was giving out such conflicting messages, acting as if he wanted her so much while at the same time planning to put as much distance between them as possible.

Petra parked her car in the hospital car park and made her way through Reception to her mother's ward.

Taking the lift up one floor, she was joined by

someone she knew—Andrea Gorton. She wasn't on her own. She was holding the hand of a small child, a little girl aged about three years old. A beautiful child with white-blonde hair and green eyes.

'How nice to see you, Mrs Gorton,' said Petra. 'You're looking well after the bone-marrow extraction. Everything still all right?'

'Oh, yes,' Andrea said heartily. 'Absolutely fine. No problem there. I was up and about in no time. By the way, this is my little granddaughter, Pip.'

Petra was nonplussed. She didn't recall Andrea having mentioned any grandchildren before.

The lift stopped and all three got out and began to walk in the same direction.

'We're just going to see Daddy, aren't we?' said Andrea, including the child in her statement. 'He's doing very well after the transplant and soon he'll be allowed home.'

'Daddy?' Petra was confused. 'You mean David Smith?'

It was only a few weeks ago that the woman had insisted almost hysterically that she wanted to have no contact whatsoever with her son. So, what was going on?

The child, trotting alongside Mrs Gorton, started chatting to Petra.

'I don't have to see Daddy through a window now,' she said excitedly. 'I can sit on a big chair next to his bed. And he can tell me stories.'

Andrea spoke in a confidential tone to Petra. 'It's so much better for the child now that my son is no longer in an isolation ward.'

Petra's jaw dropped on hearing her refer to 'my son'.

'And I've got a new granny,' said Pip. 'My first granny is in heaven and now I've got a new one.'

'That's nice,' she said, not knowing what else to say. They reached the ward where David Smith was being nursed. Pip let go of Andrea's hand and ran along to find her father's bed.

'You've changed your mind, Mrs Gorton? About keeping David a secret and not telling anyone.'

Andrea turned to her, a serene smile lighting up her face. 'It took that little girl to make me realise what's important in life and what isn't. David's wife came to visit me shortly after the transplant. She wanted to thank me even though, God knows, I didn't need thanking. She brought Pip along with her. That little girl has probably saved my sanity. I was immediately struck by a family likeness…she's the very image of my only sister who died in childhood. And then I realised she was my granddaughter and that, although I'd lost one child by giving him away, this child was in a sense also mine. How could I walk away from her as well? What kind of hard-hearted person would that make me?'

Petra impulsively put her arms around her.

'I'm so pleased,' she said. 'But what about your husband—does he know?'

'Yes, and he's thrilled to bits to find out that he's a step-grandfather! He took my confession about having an illegitimate child in his stride. He said just what you said he would. That it didn't matter two hoots any more and if anything it would only raise his credibility within the party and the con-stituency!'

'That's great news,' said Petra, and then she

watched the matronly figure of the newly discovered granny follow in the direction of her granddaughter.

Three days later, Petra's mother was discharged from hospital. She was very grateful that her daughter had taken the time off work to look after her.

'Your father's a wonderful help, but it's nice to have a daughter to chat with at a time like this,' she said one day. 'Anyway, what with all this mini-stroke thing there hasn't been time for me to ask how things are with you.' Mrs Phillips was sitting in her dressing-gown, having a cup of tea with Petra. She'd been home several days now and was making remarkable progress.

'I'm fine,' said Petra, nibbling on a delicious, crumbly, home-made biscuit.

'Your father told me that Mark's mother brought these round. That was kind of her, wasn't it? She's very embarrassed about the broken engagement, you know. Feels it was all Mark's fault. She says that you've been an absolute angel over the whole episode.'

'It was just one of those things,' said Petra. 'No one was to blame.' It suddenly occurred to her that she hadn't given a thought to Mark or the broken engagement in days. Whereas Adam was a completely different matter. He was on her mind constantly as she battled with conflicting emotions.

She was in love with him, she couldn't deny it. And if her father hadn't phoned about her mother being taken to hospital, she knew beyond a doubt that she and Adam would have made love that evening on the rug in front of the fire. She'd wanted him so much and she knew that he'd wanted her just as much. But for her it would have been a fulfilment of her love for him, a giving of herself completely and unconditionally. He didn't even have to promise marriage, but he did have to promise love. And she thought he had. She truly believed she was the one he'd been referring to when he'd told her, 'I've been in love. I still am.'

But she must have been wrong. Very wrong. For how can you profess to love someone and at the same time be making plans to leave? He was acting a role, just as surely as Porky Paterson in *Jackson's Market*. Adam was so convincingly good they should have given him an Equity card!

'Another cup of tea?' asked Petra's mother.

'No, thanks, Mum. And I think you ought to be getting back to bed again. Lots of rest, remember.'

'Yes, Doctor,' said her mother, obediently gathering her robe around her.

'I must say, you're a very good patient. You do exactly what you're told!'

'With two doctors living in the same house, watching your every move, there's very little chance of doing otherwise! But seriously, Petra, darling, I do appreciate you being here.'

'Wouldn't dream of being anywhere else.' Petra smiled at her mother, fighting back the temptation to unburden herself, to confide in her mother about Adam…her worries, her concerns.

She would have really valued her mother's opinion of the situation. Was Adam playing with her affections, or was he genuine? And if he was genuine, why was he going to work abroad when he knew that she was committed to being in Milchester? Perhaps Adam was one if those men who only wanted what they couldn't have. He had been keen enough when she'd been engaged to someone else, but had he lost interest the moment she was free?

She would love to have talked it all through with her mother, but she was very conscious of the fact that her mother's stroke had happened a very short time after the wedding had been cancelled. Her father had assured her there was no connection between the two events, but Petra wasn't taking any chances. She would keep her problems to herself and put on a happy face.

'So you don't hold a grudge against Mark?' asked her mother as Petra helped her up the stairs.

'No, not at all.'

'I'd be a lot happier if I felt there was another man in your life.'

'I'm sure there will be, Mum, given time.'

'Good. I hate thinking of you being all alone in that big city without a man to take care of you.'

'Mother! I'm a qualified doctor. I've earned my own living and stood on my own two feet for years…and will continue to do so. I don't need a man to support me, you know!'

Her mother turned and gazed at her with wise eyes. 'I'm not talking about supporting you, Petra. I'm talking about loving you.'

'Is there a Mrs Phillips living here?' asked the florist's delivery girl, clutching an enormous bunch of flowers.

'There certainly is,' replied Petra's father, taking the bouquet and bringing it into the living room where his wife was sitting, dressed warmly for her first full day out of bed.

'More flowers!' she exclaimed delightedly. 'My

friends have been so kind. The house looks like the Chelsea Flower Show! They really shouldn't.'

Petra came into the room with a cup of coffee for her mother. She admired the latest floral gift. 'People want to show you how much they care about you. You're always the first to send flowers to your friends when they've been ill. Who's this bunch from?'

Mrs Phillips reached for her spectacles in order the read the wording on the card. She looked puzzled.

'Who's Adam Driscoll?' she asked. 'I wonder if these flowers were meant for someone else?'

The unexpected mention of Adam's name made Petra's heart skip a beat.

'The delivery girl definitely said Mrs Phillips,' recalled her father.

'I suppose they might be for me,' said Petra in a small, embarrassed voice.

Her parents looked at her with interest.

'You know this person?' her mother asked. 'This Adam Driscoll?'

Petra nodded. 'He's one of my partners at the medical centre,' she said, placing the coffee-cup on a small table next to her mother. 'I introduced him to you, Dad, at the hospital.'

'Ah, yes,' said Dr Phillips. 'I remember him now. Nice young man.'

'Perhaps he's the new man in Petra's life,' said Mrs Phillips. 'I do hope so. You'd better read this to see if they were meant for you.' She handed the card to Petra.

After a brief scan of the words written on the card she didn't know whether to be pleased or disappointed. 'They're definitely for you, Mum,' she said reading the rest of the message. 'It says, "All good wishes for a speedy recovery." See.' She showed the card first to her mother and then to her father for added emphasis.

'How very kind of him,' said Mrs Phillips.

'Clever man, this Adam Driscoll,' he said, winking widely at his wife. 'One of the best ways of getting round a young lady is to make a fuss of the mother. Always works!'

'Did you send *my* mother flowers?' asked Mrs Phillips. 'I don't remember you turning up with anything as lovely at this.' She breathed in the delicate scent.

'Your dear mother had a very sweet tooth, I seem to recall. A small box of chocolates now and again never did me any harm, in her eyes at least.'

'You old schemer!' Mrs Phillips laughed. 'I'd no idea you men got up to such tricks!' She reached up to her husband for him to help her out of the cushioned softness of the settee. 'I'll go and put these in a vase of water. They really are very lovely. And I'll appreciate them even more now that I know they're from Petra's young man.'

'He's not my young man!' Petra exploded. 'He's just a good friend…not a *boyfriend*. And he won't be staying at the practice for very much longer, so it would be a big mistake to get involved with him. I've had enough problems getting involved with the wrong man, namely Mark. I'm hardly likely to want to put myself in the same position again…jumping straight out of the frying-pan into the fire!'

There was a moment's stunned silence after Petra's unexpected outburst.

'Well, then,' said her father with false jollity, 'talk-

ing of frying pans, how about those bacon sandwiches you promised to make for lunch, Petra?'

Adam sprang another surprise on her a few hours
later when he turned up in person at her parents'
front door.

'I was just passing, so I thought I'd call in,' he
said. He must have realised how improbable that
sounded but his smile didn't flicker for a moment.

Petra had answered the door. After getting over
her initial shock, she picked up on it.

'Just passing? This is hardly on your way to anywhere, I would have thought. Several miles out of
your way, to be precise!'

Part of her was thrilled to see him, as always. She
would never be able to stop herself reacting instantly
to his presence. But she willed her mind to stay calm
and didn't give in to her natural instinct, which was
to fling her arms around his neck and kiss him. She
knew she had to distance herself from the man. How
else was she going to stop herself loving him?

Adam waved an arm in the direction of his car
which was parked a short distance from the house.

'I've got my sister and little nephew with me.
We've come out for a bit of country air, thought it
would do us all good. There's a country park nearby
and so, hey, presto, here we are!'

'So you are,' replied Petra, undecided about what
her next move should be. 'Oh, I nearly forgot. The
flowers were lovely. My mother was delighted. It
was a very kind thought, thank you.'

'Don't mention it,' he said. 'How is she doing?'

'Fine,' said Petra. 'I'll be back at work on
Monday.'

'The week seemed a very long one without you,' said Adam. 'I missed you.'

There was a pause.

He's waiting for me to say, 'And I've missed you,' thought Petra. But I'm not going to say it.

'Anyway,' he said, 'we wondered if you'd like to join us. I'm sure your parents can spare you for a little while.'

'I don't think so,' she said abruptly. 'I'd better not be away for too long. I've got some ironing to do.'

'That's a shame. Chrissie, my sister, was really looking forward to meeting you. And my nephew has been practising saying "Petra" for the last half hour. He's even mastered "Adam" especially for you. You know how his mispronunciation, calling me "Dadda", caused that misunderstanding between us! Danny will be really disappointed.'

'Danny?' queried Petra.

'My nephew.' Adam turned in the direction of the parked car. A small face was pressed up against the passenger window and a little hand waved enthusiastically.

It melted her resolve. 'I suppose I could spare an hour,' she said. 'I won't come to the country park, but perhaps we could just have a drink at the village pub. They have a room where they allow children. I'll just tell my folks where I'm going and grab a jacket.'

She stuck her head round the living-room door. 'Just popping out for a drink with a friend,' she said. 'I won't be too long.'

'Stay as long as you like,' said her mother, glancing up from her knitting. 'Who did you say it was?'

'Adam Driscoll. He was passing by.'

'That name rings a bell,' said her mother, casting her mind back.

'He's the one who sent you the flowers. The one Petra says she's not going to get involved with,' said her father in his usual booming voice.

Petra shut the living-room door and was surprised to see that Adam was still waiting on the front doorstep with the door wide open. She'd imagined that he'd walked back to the car to wait for her. Her father's voice carried a long way…she just hoped it hadn't carried as far as the front doorstep. In any event, Adam gave no indication that he'd heard the remark as they walked to the car together.

'Can I have some crisps as well as a fizzy orange?' asked Danny at the Church Inn as Adam was taking their order for drinks.

'Of course you can,' said Adam. 'What are indulgent uncles for if not to buy packets of crisps for their nephews?'

As Adam went off in the direction of the bar, with Danny trotting by his side Chrissie began chatting with Petra.

'I feel as if I've known you almost as long as Adam has,' she said. 'He's always talking about you.'

'We do work well together,' conceded Petra.

'I listen to you both on the radio phone-in,' said his sister. 'That's why it's so nice to meet you in person. Adam's told you about our situation, has he?'

'About the bone-marrow transplant? Yes. But only recently. He kept it very low key,' replied Petra.

'He saved Danny's life,' said Chrissie. 'I'll always be grateful to him for that. And the nice thing is that it seems to have made a very strong bond between

Adam and Danny. Danny's too young to appreciate what's been going on but he knows that Adam is a very special person.' She glanced across the room to where Adam and Danny were standing. 'He's marvellous with children, have you noticed that?'

'Chrissie, it sounds as if you're trying to sell your brother to me,' joked Petra, who was beginning to feel this little talk was a set-up.

Chrissie blushed. 'I'm not really trying to sell him to you. But I know he likes you very much and I do so want him to be happy. He deserves to find the right woman. And from the way he talks about you—'

'I'm sorry to disappoint you, Chrissie,' interrupted Petra, 'but I don't think romance is on the cards.'

Chrissie's face fell. 'Oh, dear. I thought you liked him. Adam seems to think you do.'

'I *do* like him,' said Petra guardedly. 'I like him very much, but I don't think there's a future for us because...' She glanced up and saw Adam and Danny making their way back to the table, Adam carrying the drinks, Danny the crisps.

The child climbed up onto a window seat that looked out across the village green. Suddenly the church bells started ringing. Danny clapped his hands in glee. 'Nice bells, nice bells!' he said.

'They must have seen us coming,' said Adam. 'Either that or there's been an invasion.'

'Really?' The expression on Chrissie's face made Adam and Petra laugh out loud.

'No, not really,' said Petra. 'It's just the bell-ringers practising. Which reminds me, talking of bell-ringers, how's Hannah now that she's back at work?'

'She found it hard going at first,' said Adam, 'but

she's come to a good arrangement with Helen—she's the locum who's been filling in for her,' Adam explained to Chrissie. 'They're going to job-share. It'll suit Hannah who wants to go part time, and Helen announced that she's pregnant and job-sharing will suit her as well.'

'Helen's pregnant! How nice, I'm really pleased for her,' said Petra. 'But that means we'll have to get someone else when...' Petra stopped in mid-sentence.

'When what?' asked Chrissie.

'Oh, nothing,' Petra prevaricated. 'Just when we need another locum, I suppose.' She had been going to say 'when Adam leaves' but she'd thought better of it. It didn't seem to be an appropriate time to be talking about Adam's departure.

'The bells sound wonderful,' said Chrissie. 'Very romantic. I always think the sound of bells across a village green puts you in mind of weddings and brides and confetti and all that kind of thing.'

Petra gazed out of the window. 'That's the church where Mark and I were going to be married in the New Year.'

'Oh, I'm so sorry I mentioned it, Petra.' Chrissie was mortified by her gaffe.

'That's all right. I'm over it now.'

The bells continued to ring out as they downed their drinks and talked about other less sensitive subjects. Danny, in the meantime, had managed to drop most of his crisps on the floor and began to pick them up with every intention of eating them, dirt and all.

Adam grabbed his arm before the crisps could reach his eager mouth. 'I'll buy you some more, Danny,' he said, leading the child by the hand.

When they were alone again Chrissie briefly touched Petra. 'Me and my big mouth,' she said apologetically. 'I'd completely forgotten that you were going to be married. And in that very church! Adam told me about your engagement being broken off.'

Petra was surprised at the amount of detail that Adam had passed on about her to his sister.

'How often do you speak to him?' she asked.

'He phones me two or three times a week. Just to check on things, you know, with Danny and everything. He's been marvellous…a real life-support system,' said Chrissie.

'You'll miss him, then, when he goes to work abroad.'

'What? Is Adam leaving again?'

The stricken look on Chrissie's face confirmed what Petra had suspected—that Adam hadn't even told his sister. What a bastard! He comes back, makes himself indispensable, and then pushes off when he's getting bored. What a way to treat his sister and the nephew he professed to love so much! But, no doubt, he'd become used to an exciting life, flying out to the world's trouble spots, living for the adrenalin rush, the buzz. Once he'd experienced the glamour of that kind of lifestyle he was hardly going to settle down to being an ordinary GP in an inner city practice…hardly going to settle down to being a husband and father.

At least Petra had been warned of his plans to jet off and had been able to do a spot of damage limitation as far as getting hurt was concerned.

The hurt was there, of course, because, without really knowing how, she'd fallen in love with him…and had come within a hair's breadth of going to bed with him. What a mistake that would have been! With hindsight she could see it would have been very foolish as it was obvious to her now that all he'd ever wanted from the relationship had been sex.

'I didn't know he was leaving—he never said anything to me,' said Chrissie, staring glumly out of the window. 'I can't believe it.'

Is that the doorbell?' said Petra's father, using the remote control to turn the sound down on the TV.

Petra breathed a heavy sigh as they both heard the insistent ring.

'Who on earth can it be at this time of night?' she asked crossly. Her mother had gone to bed at least two hours ago and both she and her father were also planning to retire to bed after they'd finished watching an American sitcom.

She would be extremely glad when today was over! Seeing Adam this afternoon had put her in a depressed mood. Working with him was going to be bad enough, but seeing him socially was ten times worse.

She'd been relieved when they'd dropped her off on their way to the country park. She'd found the hour spent in the pub a great strain—watching Adam playing 'happy families' had only made her feel even more miserable than ever. When she'd let herself in, she'd had to go through another charade for her parents' benefit, putting on a cheerful act when all she'd really wanted to do had been to go upstairs and weep into her pillow. Still, there'd be plenty of opportunity for that on Monday when she returned to Milchester.

'Would you like me to answer the door?' offered her father.

'No, it's all right, I'll go. It's probably someone lost and wanting directions.'

She switched on the outside light and opened the oak door.

'Adam!' she gasped. 'What are you doing here?'

'I've come back to speak to you.' His face looked serious, almost angry. 'There are things we need to get straight. Will you come and sit in the car while we talk? It's more private there.'

'What about Chrissie and Danny?' She craned her neck to peer over his shoulder to see the car and its occupants but he'd moved so close to her he was blocking her view.

'I took them home after the country park,' he said. 'Then Chrissie told me something and I had to come back.'

'Oh?' Petra was mesmerised by the intensity of his gaze.

'She told me about a conversation she had with you at the Church Inn. We really have to talk about this, Petra!' His voice was becoming louder.

'Shh!' she said, gesturing with her hands. 'You'll wake my mother—her bedroom's at the front of the house.'

A booming voice came from the living room. 'Everything all right, Petra?'

'Yes, Dad. It's just a friend calling round. I'm slipping out for a moment. You go to bed. I'll take my key so I won't wake you up.'

Closing the door as quietly as possible, she followed Adam down the path and into his car. He started up the engine.

'Where are we going?' she asked in alarm.

'Somewhere a little more private,' he said.

He drove a short distance up a country lane away from any houses or streetlamps. He switched off the ignition and car lights. They were in darkness apart from the eerie light cast by the moon.

'What's going on?' she asked, startled by the turn of events.

'I may well ask you the same question.' Adam's voice was low and measured. 'Ten days ago you were in my arms and holding me as if you'd never let go. I saw love in your eyes and desire in your body. You wanted me as much as I wanted you. And yet today I heard your father say, "The one Petra's not going to get involved with." I thought I might have misheard. But I know I didn't because you've suddenly gone cold towards me. You shrink from my touch. You can't bear to look me in the eye. Not only that, but you feed my sister a pack of lies about me leaving my job and going to work abroad!'

'But you are, aren't you?'

'No.'

For a moment she was speechless. How could he say that?

'Adam, you told me you were going to work abroad again when you asked me to sign your passport photographs!'

'If you remember,' he replied, 'I said I *might* go abroad, or words to that effect. I certainly did *not* say I was *definitely* going to work abroad!' He remained silent for a moment. 'For goodness' sake, Petra, do you think I'd have gone ahead and planned to leave the country without even telling my sister?'

'Oh, I see.' She laughed bitterly. 'It's your sister

you're concerned about. You weren't bothered about telling me! All I know is that you said you'd probably be going abroad sooner rather than later. It's what you said!'

'But then things changed,' he replied in exasperation. 'Your engagement to Mark was broken off…and that made all the difference in the world to me! It was the best thing that ever happened as far as I was concerned. I thought I'd made that perfectly clear.'

They sat in the dark, in silence. A warm glow began to spread throughout her body. He wasn't leaving! He wasn't leaving after all!

'Petra?' His voice was like a silken caress. 'Did you hear what I said?'

'I was convinced you were leaving. And now I can't believe you're staying!'

She leaned into him and he gathered her into his embrace.

'There was a time I felt like getting the hell out of here, that's true enough.' There was a catch in his voice.

'Was it because of me? Was it my fault?' she asked.

'It wasn't anyone's fault. If anything, it was because I'm a totally obsessive person when it comes to you. Obsessive and possessive.'

He nuzzled the top of her head, burying his face in her hair. 'I wanted you all to myself. I couldn't face the prospect of you marrying Mark…'

He kissed her, deep and long.

'Can you imagine how it would have been for me?' he said, his lips brushing against her ear. 'Constantly seeing you at the practice, knowing you were going home to Mark each night, kissing him, making love to him.'

Petra trembled involuntarily. His strong arms held her closer, tighter.

'I tried to imagine what it would be like, working with you once you were a married woman,' he said. 'I would have ended up a complete and utter wreck.'

'But Mark wanted us to live in London…'

'I never really believed that he could have persuaded you to move there, you were so committed to Milchester.'

'That's true.'

'So I'd have been forced to see you almost every day and witness your happiness with another man. My jealousy would have got the better of me. I was finding it hard enough to cope with while you were just engaged to him. It would have been unbearable after you were married.'

'Poor Adam,' she said, reaching up and running her fingers through his short, thick hair. 'I'd no idea. Where would you have gone?'

'I made contact with an old colleague from my days in Bosnia. I asked him if he knew of any jobs abroad for medics. Then I found that my passport needed renewing. But I took it no further after you broke off the engagement. I just lived in hope that there was a chance for us…a chance that you might love me as much as I loved you.'

'Oh, Adam!' She clung to him, never wanting to let him go. 'I *do* love you. More than you'll ever know.'

Adam closed his eyes and almost laughed with relief. 'You do? Say it again.'

'I love you,' she murmured softly against his

cheek. 'You don't know how miserable I've been since I saw that passport envelope on your hall table. I truly believed you were going ahead with it.'

'The passport? Sure, I went ahead with it…which is just as well. I'm hoping I'll be needing it in the not too distant future.'

'But you said—'

'How do you feel about a New Year wedding in your lovely church, followed by a skiing honeymoon in Aspen?'

'This is a bit sudden, isn't it?' Petra said, trying to take it all in.

'I don't believe in long engagements,' he said. 'So, what do you think?'

'What advice would you give on your radio show?' she asked teasingly, her heart bursting with happiness.

'I'd say you should follow your natural instincts.'

'I thought you might say that.'

'I can see we're going to have to talk this over for at least an hour or two,' he said, drawing her closer to him, the warmth of his body radiating through to hers.

'Mmm,' she said, nuzzling her face against his. 'I like the idea of the hour or two, but let's not talk.'

'No, let's not.'

Modern Romance™
...seduction and
passion guaranteed

Tender Romance™
...love affairs that
last a lifetime

Sensual Romance™
...sassy, sexy and
seductive

Blaze™
...sultry days and
steamy nights

Medical Romance™
...medical drama on
the pulse

Historical Romance™
...rich, vivid and
passionate

29 new titles every month.

*With all kinds of Romance for
every kind of mood...*

MILLS & BOON®

Makes any time special™

MAT4

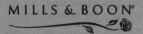

Medical Romance™

THE PERFECT CHRISTMAS *by Caroline Anderson*

Audley Memorial series

The instant, heated attraction she felt for surgeon David Armstrong made Sister Julia Revell feel acutely alive—and distinctly nervous. She couldn't put herself or her little daughter at the risk of another emotional trauma. Until a terrible event showed her how much she needed this man by her side…

THE TEMPTATION TEST *by Meredith Webber*

TV producer Jena is in Kareela Bush, Australia, to film a documentary about the hospital there, *not* to start a relationship with the handsome Dr Noah Blacklock. As both fail to resist their attraction at every turn, how long will it be before they give in to temptation once and for all?

MISTLETOE MOTHER *by Josie Metcalfe*

When Seth turned up at a remote cottage in a snowstorm, he was surprised to see Ella—and shocked to discover she was pregnant with his child. Ella was approaching term, they were stranded, and Seth was the only gynaecologist in sight. This could be the most emotional Christmas of their lives!

On sale 7th December 2001

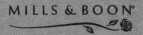

MILLS & BOON®

Medical Romance™

A CHRISTMAS TO REMEMBER by Margaret Barker

Part 3 of Highdale Practice series

Dr Nicky Devlin sees Jason Carmichael's desire for her as the perfect chance to repay him for the pain that he has caused her friend. In the run-up to Christmas she realises she loves Jason and the accusations against him turn out to be lies. How can she convince him that her feelings are real after all?

THE DOCTOR'S DILEMMA by Lucy Clark

Part 3 of The McElroys trilogy

Falling in love is definitely not on the agenda for ambitious bachelor Dr Joel McElroy. But living and working with the warm-hearted Kirsten Doyle reveals to Joel that she needs some TLC herself. With the arrival of Kirsten's orphaned niece, Joel finds himself drawing closer to this ready-made family—and facing a dilemma...

THE BABY ISSUE by Jennifer Taylor

Part 2 of A Cheshire Practice series

Practice Nurse Anna Clemence has tried to keep her pregnancy from gorgeous Dr Ben Cole, but in his desire to get closer to her, he discovers a closely guarded secret. Now he has to convince Anna that he can love this baby who is biologically neither his nor hers.

On sale 7th December 2001

Available at most branches of WH Smith, Tesco, Martins, Borders, Eason, Sainsbury's and most good paperback bookshops.

1101/03b

0801/123/MB19

OTHER NOVELS BY

PENNY JORDAN

POWER GAMES

POWER PLAY

CRUEL LEGACY

TO LOVE, HONOUR & BETRAY

THE HIDDEN YEARS

THE PERFECT SINNER

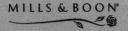

MILLS & BOON®

4 Books
and a surprise gift!

We would like to take this opportunity to thank you for reading this Mills & Boon® book by offering you the chance to take FOUR more specially selected titles from the Medical Romance™ series absolutely FREE! We're also making this offer to introduce you to the benefits of the Reader Service™—

★ FREE home delivery
★ FREE gifts and competitions
★ FREE monthly Newsletter
★ Books available before they're in the shops
★ Exclusive Reader Service discounts

Accepting these FREE books and gift places you under no obligation to buy; you may cancel at any time, even after receiving your free shipment. Simply complete your details below and return the entire page to the address below. **You don't even need a stamp!**

YES! Please send me 4 free Medical Romance books and a surprise gift. I understand that unless you hear from me, I will receive 6 superb new titles every month for just £2.49 each, postage and packing free. I am under no obligation to purchase any books and may cancel my subscription at any time. The free books and gift will be mine to keep in any case.

MIZEB

Ms/Mrs/Miss/Mr ....Initials..
BLOCK CAPITALS PLEASE

Surname..

Address...

....

....Postcode ....

Send this whole page to:
UK: The Reader Service, FREEPOST CN81, Croydon, CR9 3WZ
EIRE: The Reader Service, PO Box 4546, Kilcock, County Kildare (stamp required)

Offer not valid to current Reader Service subscribers to this series. We reserve the right to refuse an application and applicants must be aged 18 years or over. Only one application per household. Terms and prices subject to change without notice. Offer expires 31st May 2002. As a result of this application, you may receive offers from other carefully selected companies. If you would prefer not to share in this opportunity please write to The Data Manager at the address above.

Mills & Boon® is a registered trademark owned by Harlequin Mills & Boon Limited.
Medical Romance™ is being used as a trademark.